Secrets, Lies and Champagne Highs

Jeanette Hubbard

PROMONTORY
PRESS

Promontory Press
www.promontorypress.com

ISBN: 978-1-927559-76-5

Typeset by One Owl Creative in 13pt Bembo
Cover design by Marla Thompson of Edge of Water Design
Champagne Glasses created by L. Pence from the Noun Project
Cork created by Buena Buena from the Noun Project

Printed in Canada
0987654321

Dedication

To Sandy, for laughing. And for saving me from that whole standing-on-the-street-corner-with-a-cardboard-sign thingy. Thank you.

Secrets, Lies and
Champagne Highs

Chapter One

"Bloody Hell." Claudie O'Brien gave a frustrated huff and stared out the windshield of the parked BMW. Her breath was beginning to cloud the glass. On this cold winter day she was working on a Champagne cork that was dry and stubbornly clinging to the neck of the bottle. It was provoking and threatened her carefully orchestrated scenario. She gave it one last concerted twist and it moved a fraction but then stopped. It was no use. She wasn't going to get it out. She huffed loudly again and sat looking at the light snow coming down. She was not going to allow the silly cork to disrupt her final moments. She flung the bottle down on the floor by the brake and gas pedals. Fortunately she had planned with care and she had a back-up bottle. In fact, she had two but the third bottle was quite inferior and normally she wouldn't have even used it in a fruit punch. But she didn't think if she made it to the third bottle that she would notice the cheap quality. By that time if the pills and alcohol weren't working she could always get out and lay down by the river. The cold would finish her off. She fished the second bottle out of the small wicker basket on the driver's seat. This cork twisted enough that she could start rocking it back and forth, slowly working it out of the bottle. With just the slightest sigh it eased out and the car filled with the yeasty scent. It was like Christmas had come early.

She pulled the Waterford champagne flute out of the wicker basket and poured carefully so the bubbling foam didn't spill out of the glass. She was skilled at this. When the initial bubbles subsided she took her first sip and yes, it was excellent. Slightly nutty with just a hint of pear. Colder than what was recommended but she liked it that way. She nestled back contentedly in the down quilt she was tucked into and drank the first glass while she watched the river churn by outside the windshield. The CD player was playing a Vaughan Williams piece that she loved. It was just a perfect party.

Her mind flitted from memory to memory. She used to camp in this area every summer long ago with groups of friends and then, in the last several years, just by herself and her dog. The dog died and the camping came to an end. She missed it.

She poured another glass and welcomed the lassitude seeping into her limbs. It wasn't until her fourth glass that she opened the bottle of Percocet. They looked a little fuzzy. They had been sitting in her medicine cabinet for a few years since she sprained her ankle. Maybe she shouldn't have tossed the stupid silica packet that they put in all these pill bottles to absorb moisture. She shrugged. So what if they had lost a little potency? She planned on taking all of them. They should still blend nicely with the champagne and she was sure that it was this lively combination that did the trick for Marilyn. But she hadn't emulated Monroe's nudity. It had been a long time since she had a body worth seeing naked and it was too chilly in the car. She popped the first two pills and then leaned over to turn the car heater back on. In the process the entire bottle of pills sprinkled out into the driver's foot well.

"Bloody Hell." She leaned down further to pick out the white pills scattered among the leaves and grit on the floor, and in the process she knocked the discarded champagne bottle back against the brake pedal. The jarring caused the bubbles and pressure to suddenly surge against the recalcitrant cork and, with an explosive pop, the cork shot out and plugged Claudie on her right temple, causing her a split second of intense pain before she passed out.

Peter steered the pick-up truck down the last stretch of gravel road to the small campground by the Metolius River. There was a light dusting of snow and he could see in the failing light the tire tracks of TJ's rig. TJ and the other two guys were probably on their second six-pack and already prepared to give him grief for being late. If he didn't want to be ribbed all weekend about being pussy-whipped, he would need to come up with an excuse other than the sorry truth that he'd had another fight with Chrystal. Not that they would believe him. Chrystal had made it clear to them all what she thought about a bunch of men in the woods with guns. Drinking beer and shooting Bambi was another indication of the low station in life that he had sunk to. And don't get her started on the scum that were his friends. He'd made the mistake of letting her drive him over to TJ's once for his poker game with the guys. She had insisted on coming inside to say hi. She'd sized up the ambience of spilled beer, cigar smoke, and dirty socks in a split second. TJ had offered her a beer but she wouldn't even sit down. Later she'd said the sofa looked like something you put on the curb with a free sign and some yahoo picked it up to put on his trashy porch where he could sit drinking Budweiser and scratching his balls. Peter's friends were all bears with furniture.

The grief he got from the guys started when they asked him when his mommy was going to pick him up and concluded finally when they pointed out he had violated the rule to never ever bring a woman to the poker game. They were right of course. It was just that Chrystal had whined and pestered him for months. She wanted to see what was so exciting that he would leave her once a month alone with "his" kids when she couldn't even get him to take her to a nice restaurant in Bend once in a while. Well, now she knew he preferred to sit around in a stinky old RV drinking beer and talking about football. She told him then in that case she wasn't going to wash his stinking tobacco-smelling clothes when he got home.

He smiled to himself. Despite her incessant harassment he continued to play poker and he went hunting every fall. It was a small victory and he clung to it even if he no longer liked to hunt. The only shooting he did now was with an old Canon camera that his dad gave him. He didn't imagine that he was a very good photographer but he liked the way it made him really look at the world and observe the small stuff happening all around. Once he told her that he liked it because it slowed him down and she cracked that if he slowed down any further they would have to put a pacemaker in him to keep his heart going.

He pulled into the campground and could see TJ's RV parked at the far end. He drove slowly but even so almost didn't notice the old BMW parked in one of the riverside spaces. He could see exhaust coming out of the tailpipe but it was too dark to see inside the car. It seemed odd. The snow was still coming down lightly but if it came down much more the car would have a problem getting out to the main road.

Not his problem, he hoped. He wasn't interested in towing some idiot on his rare weekend off. Since he had been laid off from his position as vice-principal at Sisters' high school he had been working two jobs. The main one was as a tow-truck operator and in the summer he did some landscaping. It was the Central Oregon cliché—two jobs with a view. Only he didn't have much of a view at his house.

Inside TJ's RV the generator was going and the heat was cranked up. The guys were stripped down to tee shirts and the room was littered with coats, boots, half-lit cigars, and beer cans. They were huddled over gun scopes, laser bore-sighters, magazines, and clips. TJ was leading a vigorous discussion about the merits of Sako versus Remington rifles. The catcalls and ribbing that Peter had expected were half-hearted and subsided by the time he chucked his coat and opened his first beer.

TJ was the designated cook for the first night. He had his traditional bland chili bubbling on the stove, adding to the heat and humidity in the small space. It had been suggested on several occasions that perhaps he should switch to spaghetti or something else since it was apparent that he in fact did not like or use much chili pepper in his chili. He claimed it was the only dish he knew but as a concession to the others he had started to bring several bottles of hot sauce to be applied as desired. Peter had fruitlessly suggested anything without beans would be nice, but he was generally shouted down as a wuss. It was an early night for the group. They planned on being up at first light so shortly after dinner they crashed. Peter, being the last to arrive, sacked out on the miniscule sofa and cracked a window for air not suffused with chili bean gas. He zipped his sleeping bag tight as the temperature finally dropped to the low teens outside and the trailer lost its residual heat.

With a stomach wrestling with chili, garlic bread, and beer, he tried to get comfortable. For some reason the sofa seemed shorter than last fall. He shifted several more times and then sat up. It was going to be a long night. He grabbed his coat and stepped outside to take a piss; his breath fogged in the freezing air. The snow had stopped and a few stars were visible in the sky. And just above the sound of the river was the faint sound of a car engine. Unbelievable. That stupid car was still there and the engine was still on. The idiot was going to run out of gas before he had a chance to kill himself by running off the road.

Peter was telling himself not to get involved as he slowly crunched through the dry snow towards the now powdery white car. He hesitated, then knocked on the driver's window. The snow slid off and he peered in. The seat had a small basket sitting on it. There was just a jumble on the passenger seat, which looked like a sleeping bag. He stood and looked around. There were no footprints other than his own around the car. He walked around to the passenger side and brushed the snow off to get a better look at the pile on the seat. It was still too dark but something didn't look right. He tried the handle to the car and it opened with just a slight frosty tug. He bent down and pushed down on the lump and, with a heart-snapping start, realized it was a body.

"Oh Christ." He shook it gently but got no response. Then with dread he slipped a glove off and reached around to feel if the body was cold. His hand connected with a face that seemed warm but the car had the heat jacked up. He pressed two fingers under the jaw and waited to see, yes, there was a pulse. Not strong but it was there. He pulled the body up. It was a woman and she was sticky with wine. Beneath a large bruise on her forehead her eyes fluttered briefly and he thought she looked at him. Her lips moved and he leaned down to hear what she was saying.

"Fuck off." Her eyes closed.

"Shit." Swearing softly, he walked back to his pick-up and started it. Inside the trailer he tried to wake TJ, who was a deputy sheriff, but he was out cold. One of the other guys roused and Peter quickly told him what was going on. With a minimum of grumbling, his friend rolled out of his sleeping bag and followed Peter out. He helped Peter get the old lady into the pick-up and then he went back to bed. Peter drove carefully out of the campground; yes indeed, it was going to be a very long night.

Chrystal had just finished her Zumba routine and started

preparing her special cleansing smoothie when the phone rang. She checked the caller ID before picking up. It was her mother who was on another cruise. Earlier in the month it had been the eastern Caribbean, and now it was the Gulf of Mexico. Since Elaine McGruder's third husband had dumped her she hadn't been able to stay put for more than the time to book the next trip.

"Hello mother, are you calling to gloat? Where are you now?"

"Belize. You could have come with me. It's early enough in the cruise season, I'm sure I could have gotten us a larger suite. I just can't bear to think of you forced to take care of those ungrateful brats while your beastly husband is off playing Daniel Boone."

Chrystal could hear the ice cubes in her mother's cocktail glass and there was a brief pause as she took another drag on her cigarette. Despite Chrystal's scolding about the damage caused by smoking, drinking, and the sun, her mother persisted indulging in all three. She told her daughter life was too short to avoid the things she loved and, besides, God made Botox and plastic surgeons for a reason. As far as Chrystal could see, the surgeons were barely able to keep her mother on the shady side of her true chronological age.

"I would've loved to have joined you if I hadn't just landed this job at Six Firs. I would have come in a New York minute." Chrystal took a gulp of the greenish concoction that she had just poured from the blender. The kitchen counter was littered with stray bits of vegetables and there was an empty packet of Dr. Ray's miracle anti-oxidant rejuvenating powder. It was the powder that had turned perfectly respectable blended carrots, cauliflower, and tomatoes into the disagreeable green and slightly gummy concoction that Chrystal was gamely chugging.

"That's another thing. It is just disgraceful that man can't even support you and that you have to work a second job at a restaurant wearing some hideous uniform and slinging hamburgers and fries. I shudder to think what it's doing to your complexion and hair."

"You know that Six Firs isn't a hamburger joint, Mother. It's the finest destination resort in Central Oregon. And I'm not slinging anything. I'm the evening hostess and I get to wear a lovely black dress and heels. I never have to go into the kitchen unless I want to grab a shrimp salad before my shift. The waitresses and waiters are all trailer trash of course but I keep my interactions with them purely professional."

"Still, when do you think the real estate market is going to rebound? You'd think it would be recovering by now."

"I'm hoping that by next spring things will pick up. But don't you see? That's the beauty of working at the Resort. I'm meeting new people who might be interested in resettling in our wonderful sunny climate and I'm rubbing elbows with some local heavyweights who might give me some referral business. I'm going to make important contacts if I play my cards right."

"I hope you're right, dear. By the way, I was sorry to hear about Peter's Aunt Minnie."

"God, that was a blow. We just got the zoning variance approved for the garage conversion and she ups and strokes out on us."

"Well she was eighty-three, dear. Quite remarkable considering her vodka consumption. All those Walker sisters were lushes, you know. What are you going to do now? Do you have to prove that she's really living there?"

"She needed to live there two years to make the variance permanent. I'd probably get away with it if it wasn't for that snoop Mrs. Fowler. She actually had the nerve to write in an objection to the county."

"Why? What's it to her?"

"She said it would lower property values and place an additional burden on the community well. She's crazy. The whole reason I wanted the apartment was to increase the value of this place. Peter's house is small and so … average. With a guesthouse or additional rental unit, the market value will go up. In a couple of years we could sell and move someplace decent."

"I hope you're right. Has Peter been looking for any other type of work? Or is he relying on you to keep everything afloat?"

"Please, Peter works hard. It's not his fault they slashed school funding. When he was vice-principal he made decent money and we had a little social standing."

"Yeah but being a tow-truck driver doesn't open many doors now, does it? Tell me, has Dr. Ray been in touch? He said he was going to check out Central Oregon to see if the harmonics or whatever would be conducive for his next transformational retreat center. I tell you, that man could look into the very depths of my soul, Chrystal. He awakened things in me that I never knew existed. I hope that you get a chance to meet him."

"Yes well … oops, Maddie just got home. I'll call you later." Chrystal put down the phone and finished her health drink. She had already met the electrifying Dr. Ray. And she had devised a plan that she didn't want to discuss with her mother. She heard the front door open and the plunk of a heavy book bag being dropped by the door despite her insistence that all school crap go upstairs immediately. The footsteps coming down the hall were soft and kind of creeping, and then a mass of brown curls topping a teenage girl's cautious face appeared. She was obviously hoping to find the kitchen empty. Chrystal forced herself to smile and indicated the island stool. Her attempts to guide Maddie weren't any more pleasant for her than they were for the girl. But damn, the girl needed a lot of help. She would never survive high school if she didn't start paying attention to what was important. She dressed like a street kid in some godforsaken third world country.

"Plop yourself down, Maddie. I just whipped up one of my special concoctions. Chock full of vitamins and all sorts of good things for that complexion of yours. You want me to fix one for you?"

"Uh no." Maddie's hand tentatively touched her face, searching for any new outbreaks. She pulled out a Costco container of lasagna and started reading the instructions under Chrystal's disapproving look.

"You know, Madeleine, all that dairy and meat will put years on your face over time."

"I'm fourteen, Chrystal. I want to look older." She left the "duh" off the end of the sentence but Chrystal heard it loud and clear.

In her perkiest voice, she said, "How was school? I noticed that you didn't wear the new dress I bought you. Was it too tight? Do we need to let the waist out a little?"

Maddie didn't answer. Chrystal realized she was being ignored. Giving up on the hopeless attempt to help the girl, she resumed staring at the worthless garage.

Maddie shifted from one foot to the other, trying to concentrate on the cooking instructions and blocking the chirping coming out of her stepmother's mouth. She couldn't figure out why Chrystal couldn't just let her be. She was comfortable in the baggy jeans and sweatshirts she always wore; they were her signature. No one at school messed with her. She slipped under the radar because she didn't try to compete on the prissy girly level that Chrystal apparently thought was vital to middle school success. Look where it got her. A lame job as a real estate agent that she was clearly not making a go of and an even lamer job now at that tourist crap restaurant.

Maddie glanced up to see Chrystal staring out the window at the empty converted garage, a thin green line crusting her upper lip. She wondered if she could snap a picture with her cell phone without the dumb twit noticing.

After the trip to the hospital Peter was too tired to drive back to the campground. Although the prospect of going home and having to rehash the whole hunting Bambi argument with Chrystal did not appeal to him, sleeping in his own bed was more enticing than TJ's miniscule couch. He let himself into the house and quietly checked on the kids first. Sam was buried under the blankets so completely that Peter had to touch the lump to make sure there was a body there. His son was warm and alive. He thought of the old woman for a moment. What led her to that choice? He would never know. He turned off the TV and Wii Sam had left on. Then he poked his head into Maddie's room. She glanced up from her tablet and smiled. One of her feet was keeping a beat to the music coming from her iPod. He pointed to his watch and she mouthed "okay." He didn't linger to make sure she turned it off. It was Friday, not a school night. His bedroom was empty. Chrystal should be home soon from the restaurant and he hoped she would be too exhausted to take up her anti-hunting crusade.

Chrystal was in no position to carp about hunting. In fact

she had bagged her game and her sore and exhausted feet were now pointed up at the ceiling of one of the better suites at Six Firs Resort. Dr. Ray had a firm grip on her ankles as he guided Chrystal to a higher plane of existence. She was yodeling her appreciation of his efforts in a way that would have surprised Peter had he been there, as she was much more muted during their ever more rare marital matings. With a whoop, Ray flipped her over and began pummeling from the rear, all the time trying to watch his performance in the mirror over the dresser. Chrystal would be exhausted and sore in several areas before her night's work was finished. But her plan was in motion.

Peter barely registered when Chrystal slid into bed. She didn't wake him to ask why he was home. She was chagrined when she found his truck in the driveway and had prepared an explanation that, while flimsy, would have worked; however, it was fortunate that Peter was asleep. She showered quickly and quietly climbed into bed. It took her a long time to relax. Her feet and her pussy were killing her and she was still aflutter from the wine and the excitement of the after-hours assignation. Illicit. She had never had an illicit affair, at least not one where she was the married person, not her lover. It gave her an entirely different perspective. She would have to rehearse various excuses. She didn't want to be surprised without one again. Of course, Peter was such a dork, she would have to be pretty blatant to excite any suspicion on his part. She wondered why he was home but it could wait until morning. Now probably wasn't the time to start giving him grief about being gone from home so much.

Chapter Two

Both kids were still sleeping soundly as was Chrystal when Peter got up and made a quick breakfast. But he tarried too long with coffee and the paper and Chrystal caught him before he escaped.

"Good morning, sweetie. I was so surprised to find you in bed when I got home. Did you decide not to go hunting after all?" Chrystal said this while she was nuzzling up to his back. This should have been Peter's first clue—Chrystal was not known for being a cheerful morning person.

"No, I'm going back … Something strange happened last night at the campground." He described the discovery of the old woman, that it was likely she had tried to commit suicide, and that he had taken her to the Bend hospital and dropped her off.

"You poor dear. Is she going to be all right?" Chrystal poured herself a cup of coffee and started assembling the morning's fruit ensemble for her smoothie.

"I suppose so. I didn't hang around. She was alive when I left."

He drained his cup and went to put on his coat. Chrystal seemed distracted and he wanted to get going. He peeked back into the kitchen but she was busy tossing things into the blender so he said goodbye and left. Chrystal was just as anxious that he get going as he was. She wanted to avoid any questions about what time she came home the previous evening, well, morning actually. And she liked the weekend mornings when the kids slept in. It gave her a little quiet time to think. She poured the blue liquid in a tall glass and stood at the sink pondering the empty converted garage; the one that would stay empty since they no longer had a doddering old relative to put into it. She briefly wondered if she could convince her mother to visit for a while but she nixed that thought in the bud. Her mother would refuse to look the part and under the current circumstances she didn't want her mother underfoot. Elaine McGruder would recognize her litany of evasions, half-truths, and outright lies, all of which would have to be employed if she pursued this liaison. Just thinking of it gave her a thrill. Dr. Ray was staying at Six Firs until he found a suitable house. He said he would switch real estate agents and she expected a big commission when she found him the perfect place. Even more exciting were his development plans. He talked about the consortium that he was putting together to build a spiritual retreat. If she got in on the ground floor of that then goodbye tacky ranch house and hello luxury dream home. With granite counters.

Outside the window she spied Mrs. Fowler across the street open her garage and pull out her snow blower. There were barely two inches of snow but the whole neighborhood was going to have to listen to her stupid machine as she toiled to keep her walk and driveway pristine. The old biddy started it up and let it idle for a few minutes as she put her gloves back on; all the while she was staring at Chrystal's converted garage, a pruney frown on her face.

God, Chrystal thought. If she complains that we haven't established Peter's aunt in the apartment by the end of the month then we could be forced to rip out the shower and stove, making the damn thing impossible to rent. Why couldn't she drop from a stroke? Come on snow blower, bring it on.

Upstairs Sam wakened to the sound of the snow blower and tried to untangle himself from the nest of covers. Released from the blankets, he rolled onto his back for a moment and stared at the ceiling. It was a ritual for him, a silent prayer to his dead mother. One of the few memories he had of her is her painting the sun, the moon, and the planets on the ceiling, telling him the whole time about how incredible the solar system was. She wanted to go to the stars. That's what he wanted to be, an astronaut. Right now though, he wanted something to eat, and he said another little prayer that Chrystal wouldn't be in the kitchen. She had no clue what an eight-year-old boy liked to eat for breakfast.

"What are you doing?" Sam stood in the doorway to the kitchen, puzzled by the strange waving motions Chrystal was making at the window.

"Nothing, sweetie, just trying to put a hex on Mrs. Fowler."

"What's a hex?" He climbed onto the island stool facing out the window.

"It's like a charm, honey. Do you want a blueberry smoothie? I can make it super healthy with some kale and some flax seeds? They'll make you grow big and strong."

Sam frowned, "Maybe just with blueberries. The flax seeds stick in my teeth." He watched her anxiously in case she slipped the seeds or the kale in, but she made it without the add-ons. Relieved, he took the drink and escaped into the living room. He liked Saturday morning because no one fought with him over the TV. He had complete control of the remote.

Chrystal heard the shrill blast of a sugary cereal ad and went to close the door between the kitchen and living room. Then she immediately stuck her back in to make sure Sam wasn't on the new white couch with the blueberry drink. Good little boy, he had spread the old blanket out and was sitting enthralled in front of bouncing green and blue somethings dancing on the screen.

It wasn't until she was dressing that the solution struck her. It took her ten minutes before she found her cell phone under a towel on the counter. He was nearly out of cell phone range and his voice faded a couple of times before she got the information she needed. Claudette O'Brien, at the South Bend Hospital. She hoped the old lady was still alive. If she wasn't too crazy then she was going to come in handy.

Chapter Three

Claudie came awake slowly. The bustle out in the corridor was only gradually working its way through the fog that was wrapped around her brain. Below that noise was a faint whooshing sound and when she opened her eyes she only had one thing to say and it startled the skinny nurse who was changing her IV.

"Fuck a duck." The jumpy nurse caused Claudie to focus a baleful eye in her direction. Muted light was coming in through the curtains and by squinting she could see she was in a hospital room. There was another bed next to hers with someone covered with blankets. The whooshing sound was the ventilator the person was connected to. The nurse said something to Claudie and peered deeply into her eyes before patting her on the arm and leaving.

"Water, water, you dumb cow," she croaked to the nurse's retreating back. Her mouth was sticky and her forehead hurt. She raised her hand to feel the large bump above her eyes and tubes trailed across the white sheet. How the hell did she get that? Did they drop her or something? She could sue. She wanted to sue the dumb bastard who had brought her here. Why couldn't people leave her alone?

She looked around for the call button and finally spied it on the bed stand, safely out of her reach. Her throat hurt. They wouldn't have been so silly as to pump her stomach? She would definitely have grounds for a lawsuit then. She supposed she was in Bend. Probably a second-rate hospital. If someone didn't come soon, she was going to get out of bed and make a scene. That thought perked her up, and she realized that she really didn't feel all that bad—just thirsty. The IV was probably just saline. She gingerly started peeling the tape away from the needle in the back of her hand.

"Mrs. O'Brien, what are you doing? Stop." The skinny nurse rushed to her side and smoothed down the tape. "You should call us if you need something."

"I would have if anyone with half a brain had bothered to put the call button where I could reach it. I need to go to the bathroom. And I need a glass of water. Then I need to talk to someone about getting out of here." Claudie could hear the peevishness in her voice and tried to moderate it. A small part of her realized that being crotchety with nurses rarely produced the outcomes that were desired.

The skinny nurse was satisfied that Claudie had not dislodged her IV needle and then asked, with the volume one extends to deaf and possibly delusional old biddies, "I can get you a bedpan, hon. The doctor has not signed off on you being allowed out of bed."

Claudie sputtered, "A bedpan! That's ridiculous. There's nothing wrong with my legs. I'm perfectly capable of getting up. I want to see a doctor. Now." Fuck being nice to the nurse, she thought.

What was going to be a full-scale tug of wills was interrupted by a knock on the door and Chrystal's head immediately popping around it.

"Hi!" The bright and perky word ricocheted around the room.

Claudie and the skinny nurse looked at Chrystal in her fuchsia pink coat and waited for some explanation for her sudden appearance. Chrystal stepped to the bed and in a quiet you're-in-the-hospital-like whisper asked, "Can I speak to Mrs. O'Brien in private for a few minutes?"

"Certainly," the nurse said, "I'll just go get that bedpan for her." She smiled acidly down at Claudie and then disappeared out the door.

"Who the hell are you?" Claudie hazarded a guess that this slender and smartly dressed young woman was not a hospital employee. For a moment she was alarmed that she could be a psychologist. Could they hold her against her will if they knew she tried to commit suicide? How was she going to explain the circumstances of her little riverside jaunt?

"Mrs. O'Brien, my name is Chrystal. It was my husband who rescued you last night." Claudie's frown deepened. Chrystal hurried on. "I was talking to the hospital staff about your condition and I think I can help."

"Jesus. And just what do you and the staff think is my condition? And why the hell are they talking to you about it? I'll tell you one thing, I have a few words I'd like to share with that busybody, your husband. Where the hell is he? And Jesus S. Christ, can someone get me a glass of water?" She started prying at the tape on her hand again.

"I'll get it, sweetie." Chrystal took a glass from the bed stand and gently tapped Claudie's busy hand. "Stop that. If you want them to think you're not all right in your head just keep poking at that IV and making trouble." Claudie's frown deepened as she watched Chrystal disappear into the bathroom. She quickly returned and handed the glass to Claudie, who took long fast swallows as Chrystal settled onto the adjoining bed. Claudie scowled at this cavalier attitude towards the other patient but Chrystal was oblivious. The form on the bed didn't show any signs of being affronted.

"Is that better now? Can we talk about your future?" Chrystal didn't wait for a reply. "We don't have time to explore why you were out in the middle of nowhere chugging champagne and popping pills. Maybe your cat died, your parakeet, whatever. The thing is if they think you're going to try again they're going to trundle you up and send you down to the mental hospital in Salem. You aren't planning on trying again are you?"

Claudie gave a truculent grunt and waited for the rest of the spiel. This Chrystal was not as flighty as she looked.

"My first question is do you have family who can take you in?" Claudie gave a brief negative shake of her head. "Good. I mean, bad for you—they especially don't like to release would-be suicides who don't have any family support."

"What is this to you? Are you my savior like your husband?" The frown had segued to a look of deep suspicion. Chrystal didn't look like some bible thumper but you never know.

"God, no. But I do have a proposition for you plain and simple. I can help you and you can help me. I just need you to tell the hospital that I'm your niece and that I have a place for you to stay until you feel better." Claudie viewed Chrystal's winning smile with profound misgiving.

"So you want to adopt me? You want to be my benefactor? What do you get out of it?"

So Chrystal explained her dilemma with the empty converted garage, which she had spent a fortune on renovating for her dearly departed aunt and now would have to rip out because of that miserable snoop Mrs. Fowler. That old biddy should just be put out of her misery. There was only one solution short of murder. She could offer a free place for

Claudette to stay for up to say a year? Maybe longer if things worked out. How did that sound? A free place to live in sunny Central Oregon. Wouldn't that be great?

Claudie sat in silence digesting this. She glanced uneasily at the unmoving form beside Chrystal, who followed her glance.

"Don't you worry about Corrine here. She's been in a coma since she keeled right over in the middle of Dan's cold beer aisle about a month ago." Chrystal gave Corrine a hearty pat on her knee and laughed. It was a piercing mean girl laugh that made Claudie wince. "Poor thing, all the clerks used to dive for cover whenever they saw her coming so no one noticed her on the floor for over an hour. None of her relatives want to be the one to pull the plug. They're afraid they'll be accused of spite. Anyway, she can't hear a thing." Chrystal gave the comatose old lady another pat and turned back to Claudie.

Claudie hadn't really made a contingency plan. What she needed was time to think this out. Out of the hospital was what she needed, and this clever young woman was offering her an easy way out. There would be nothing that could prevent her from moving on as soon as she wanted. And she wouldn't mind having an opportunity to explain to the husband how deeply she begrudged his interference with her exit plan.

"I think we have a deal. Now go tell that skinny nurse that I want to get out of bed and go take a pee."

The escape was not as slick as Chrystal had hoped. They had to wait for the social worker to interview them before they could sign the paperwork and leave. The only clothes that Claudie had were drenched with champagne and, as she waited sitting in the wheelchair, her body heat released the sour smell till it filled the room. The social worker wrinkled her petite nose when she finally bustled in. She was in her mid-fifties with a barrel body and stork-like legs. She was wearing a loose dress with a deeply scooped neckline and the jacket she wore over it was not up to the task of containing a generous bosom. A thin gold necklace with a single clear crystal nestled just above said bosom. Her long dense blonde curls fell below her shoulders and framed a heart-shaped face. Her voice boomed in the small room as she questioned Claudie about the circumstances of her "accident". Claudie had sufficient time while she waited to work out a plausible explanation. She had simply gone to the river to mourn the death of her cat, the pills were for her bad back, and she had only meant to take one before she spilled them. She didn't know why she had blacked out or why she had a bump on her head. This last part was true. No, she didn't have a history of blacking out.

Mrs. Boyle the social worker hesitated. There was something off about the old woman and her niece. She couldn't put her finger on it but the story seemed too innocent. But the next words out of Claudie disabused her of the notion that Claudie was a confused and benign old lady.

"My lawyer will be contacting you shortly. I expect we'll want to see the surveillance tapes from the emergency room. It is my belief that either the ambulance workers or someone on your staff dropped me. There is no other explanation for the dreadful bruise on my head. I certainly didn't fall sitting in my car and I ache all over. The first thing my niece and I are going to do is see my personal doctor. I wouldn't be surprised that your doctors missed something and I am not confident that under the circumstances that it would be in my best interest to remain here." Claudie paused to enjoy the woman's slack-jawed face and the tumult of confused thoughts racing behind her eyes.

"I will be staying with my dear niece Chrystal in Sisters. She has the contact information all written down for you. Unless there is anything else, we need to get going, I'm sure you can appreciate that I need to shower and change. Hospitals, after all, are the places you can find the most dreadful germs."

With a cheerful "Bye, bye", Chrystal handed Mrs. Boyle her card and then pushed Claudie towards the door under the gaze of the bewildered social worker.

This interview had not gone as expected. Mrs. Boyle prided herself on her ability to control difficult situations and she had just been outmaneuvered by a doddering old wino she didn't believe for a second. Now she was going to have to meet with the hospital administrator and tell him about a potential lawsuit. Darn, the investigation was going to create a lot of work. On the up side, if she could inveigle Mrs. O'Brien to sign a release and the Director thought she handled this well by averting a lawsuit, she might be up for a larger year-end bonus. Maybe she could afford that meditation retreat in Sedona next spring. She found herself whistling a little song as she headed down the corridor to the administrative offices.

Claudie ditched the wheelchair at the hospital door. The air outside was crisp and the sky had cleared overnight. A light dusting of snow on the ground was still clean and white. For an unexpected day of existence it was rather beautiful. She squinted in all the brightness and followed Chrystal to her car, an old blue Volvo with minor signs of rust on the fenders. The inside was clean at least. The driver's seat had a nice sheepskin covering but unfortunately the passenger seat was freezing cold black vinyl that crackled slightly as Claudie settled in.

"We do good together, you and I." Chrystal's voice was cloying in its cheerfulness. "We had that old buffalo on the run. She didn't look like she knew what hit her."

Claudie didn't remember Chrystal contributing much to the comeuppance of the social worker but she wasn't in the mood to argue. She wanted the car to heat up, she wanted to get where they were going, and she wanted to shower and change. Breakfast would be good. She was famished. She always was after a night of heavy drinking, although three or four glasses of champagne didn't constitute heavy drinking in her book.

She listened as Chrystal kept up a stream of chatter during the thirty-minute ride. By the time they had arrived home Claudie knew it was the second marriage for Peter. His first wife had died, leaving him with two young children who were apparently really sweet once you got to know them. Peter was a high school vice-principal until the last round of educational cuts. Now he was working as a tow-truck driver until the economy came around. Chrystal hoped the state legislators would get their heads out of their behinds soon and start funding schools like they should. Peter was on a hunting trip when he found her. Claudie noticed Chrystal skittered away from talking any more about those circumstances. Chrystal hoped Claudie would feel part of their family while she "recovered".

They pulled into the driveway of the little ranch house on the south edge of Sisters. One side of the street had small, nearly identical houses built sometime in the nineties. Across the road was an older house that looked turn of the century—not the last turn of the century. It sat back a little way on about five acres and had an old barn tucked in behind it. Chrystal's house was directly across from it. The remodeled garage was semi-detached and there was a little covered walkway connecting it to the house. Chrystal opened the side door with a cheery "ta da" and stood watching for Claudie's reaction. Claudie had concluded that Chrystal thought she was homeless and destitute, desperate for any port in the storm. She felt no need to disabuse her of that conclusion.

The apartment was freezing and Chrystal bustled around turning on the heat and lights. Claudie looked over the small living space. There was a kitchenette along the rear wall and two doors, one to a tiny bathroom and another to a small bedroom. The appliances were good, mid-range in quality, and the sink and counters were middling but okay. The furniture was used top-of-the-line Goodwill with somewhat disparate floral and plaid patterns. It would work for now. She could change anything if she wanted. Definitely that recliner would have to go; it was butt ugly and too big. She forced a big smile on her face and made appropriate notes of appreciation. All she wanted was to be alone but Chrystal wouldn't leave her be. While the apartment heated up she told Claudie that she could shower in the "big" house. Chrystal promised to rustle her up some clothes. Claudie was doubtful of that. Chrystal looked to be about a size five and it had been a couple of decades since Claudie was that small. But a warm shower would help her feel more normal, and then she could begin to figure out what to do with this unanticipated and slightly unwelcome fact of continued existence.

The housekeeper stripped the hospital bed and bent to pick up some tissues tossed on the floor when a garbled stream of profanity erupted from the woman on the other bed. She jerked up, one hand trying to hold down her wildly beating heart, and looked at the now thrashing Corrine. She grabbed the call button and pressed repeatedly until the volume of invective exceeded her sense of duty and she fled. A nurse rushed in and tried to restrain Corrine, who was not a large woman by any means, but appeared to be in a frenzy that was not easily contained.

Word spread quickly in the hospital that the coma lady had revived after almost a month. It was unheard of. Not only was Corrine Bales awake but she apparently still had the same abrasive and obscene voice that had made her infamous in the Greater Bend area. Someone was going to have to notify the relatives. Pity the poor nephew. TJ was a deputy sheriff with enough on his plate with all the county layoffs and now he would have to figure out a way to help her convalesce outside the hospital. No one paid any attention to Corrine's insistence that a murder conspiracy had been hatched in her hospital room. Her paranoid tendencies had been widely discussed by those who knew her. They all chuckled at her ever more elaborate tale of a murder plot to kill a woman because of a garage.

Chapter Four

The first thing Peter noticed when he returned from the hunting trip was the warm and enticing smell of pizza coming from the kitchen. He chucked his coat and hoped that there was some left for him. He needn't have worried. When he entered the little dining nook there were still plenty of slices on the pans. The kids looked up from the untasted slices on their plates and there was no sign of the typical pizza frenzy and joy he expected. There was a third glum face at the table, an older woman who he didn't recognize. Chrystal came in carrying three large glasses of milk.

"Honey, you're just in time for pizza. There's a vegan one with eggplant and chard and the other one is a vegan with root vegetables." She set the milk in front of the woman and the kids. "Eat up everybody before it gets cold." She went back into the kitchen and Peter could hear the pop of a cork. He knew a good glass or two of red wine would be the only thing making the pizza tolerable.

Sam took a tentative nibble and then set it down, Maddie was carefully picking the vegetables off her slice, and the old woman was staring at the glass of milk with an arched eyebrow.

"There's not even real cheese on this, Dad." Maddie was staring at the denuded slice of pizza crust. "If you can't get her to feed us food instead of this crap then I'm going to start begging to stay over at Millie's for supper. Pleeeeze do something."

An argument within the first fifteen minutes of coming home was something that Peter had hoped to avoid. He took a twenty out of his pocket and handed it to Maddie.

"Go to Mad Dog Pizza quickly." Maddie bolted, pulling Sam along with her. The old woman looked a little wistfully at their retreating backs.

"I'm sorry, I don't think we've met. I'm Peter."

"Yes, I've been looking forward to meeting you again."

Peter didn't think she said this with pleasure and he was taken aback by the decidedly unfriendly look the woman gave him. Maybe he had met her, a student's mother? Before he could pursue it Chrystal returned with two full glasses of red wine and looked at the empty chairs and deserted pizza slices. She frowned but didn't say anything. She handed Peter a glass and didn't notice the avid look on Claudie's face.

"You remember Claudie O'Brien. She's going to be staying for a while in the apartment." Chrystal sat and began to serve herself some of the pizza and failed to see the dawning shock suffuse Peter's face. It didn't pass by Claudie.

"Chrystal, I need to have a word with you." He gave her arm a little tug and went into the living room. He shut the door after her and then hissed as quietly but forcefully as he could, "Are you insane?" There was much emphasis on the 'insane'.

"What?" Chrystal appeared innocently surprised by his alarm.

"You brought that woman into our home, around my children? What were you thinking? Who knows what she could do next?"

"Oh don't be silly, Peter, she's fine. She has gone through a rough patch and I couldn't stand the thought of her all alone in that hospital."

"The hospital is where she needs to be. She's sick. Normal people don't try to kill themselves with pills and booze. She's probably an alcoholic. God knows what else she's on."

"Peter, we don't really know that she tried to kill herself. She says it was an accident. And we need her. She'll be in the apartment most of the time. All the time. We can keep an eye on her. She won't be around the kids at all. Please, if we don't have an old lady in there by the end of next week the county will revoke our special use permit. We'll have to completely gut it and return it back to a garage. All that money and work for nothing!"

"My children are more important than that stupid apartment."

"Yes, of course. More important than me or my needs, I know that. Oh boy do I know that; I'm a second class citizen in the Walker household."

Peter felt a sudden lurch as the discussion charged off once again in the quagmire of blended family politics. Chrystal was a take-no-prisoners champion in this arena. He could see that she had even managed to squeeze out a few tears—the ultimate weapon.

In the dining nook Claudie had appropriated Peter's glass of wine and sat trying to decide whether to intervene or quietly slip back to her apartment. Emotions were a little too volatile for her taste and it was clear that the poor husband who, even Claudie admitted had a legitimate concern, was now going to be twisted into a pretzel by the clever Chrystal. She stood up and topped off her glass of wine and let herself out the backdoor. Chrystal had things under control and as long as Claudie lay low Peter could be pacified. She stood outside for a few minutes; the night sky was clear and chock full of stars. She was filled with the wonder of it all. For the first time since her 'accident' she felt content to be alive. She let herself into her little apartment; it could be made quite sweet.

If she decided to stay she could tweak it. A few changes and it would be perfect. It would do until she made up her mind.

Chapter Five

"Hey, Maddie, look what the 'Coly' is doing now." Sam stood at the kitchen sink eating a toaster waffle and looking out the window.

"I don't care what the crazy old lady is doing. Dad said to keep away from her." Maddie was searching through papers on the little desk area by the refrigerator. She'd seen Chrystal pull a small pink slip from the pile the previous night. It looked like the twit had written down some of her passwords and left it next to where she usually dumped her laptop. And there on the bottom was a small pink page. This was going to make things a whole lot easier.

"Okay, but she's trying to push Dad's chair out her door."

Maddie joined him at the window and they watched as Claudie first pushed, and then, clambering over the recliner in the doorway, tried to pull the chair through. It was now firmly wedged in the doorjamb.

Maddie grabbed her jacket and shoved her feet into her boots. She ran out and stood across from Claudie who had climbed back into her apartment.

"What are you trying to do? This is my dad's chair. You can't just push it outside. Who gave you permission?"

Claudie stared at the agitated young girl for a minute. She had not spent any time around a teenager since she had been one herself. She had no fond memories of that time in her life. Now there was an angry one standing at her door.

"The thing is, Maddie, I'm getting a new chair and there won't be room for both of them. Maybe we can get your dad to put it back in your house."

"He can't. Chrystal won't let him. That was his favorite chair until she wanted new furniture. Why can't you two like chairs that are comfortable? We can't even sit on anything in the living room. She bought a white couch for the living room. Who does that? And the carpet's white too." The pitch of Maddie's little diatribe ended with a wail and there were incipient tears that Claudie found quite alarming. She didn't have the energy to fight the chair and a hysterical teenager.

"Okay Maddie. If you can help me, you shove and I can pull, we can get the chair back inside and then we can sit down and discuss this. Away from prying eyes." Claudie glanced significantly across the street to where the curtains in Mrs. Fowler's windows had twitched back a few inches. Maddie started to push and Sam joined her in a half a minute. They succeeded in getting the chair unstuck and back inside the apartment. The children stood awkwardly in the doorway, surveying the interior. It didn't look much changed from when Chrystal had set it up. The furniture was all from their family room before Chrystal started remodeling and refurnishing their home. Sam walked over to the old plaid sofa and sat down. It was well-loved territory where movies and popcorn could be consumed without fear of spills or recrimination.

Claudie was non-plussed by this. She didn't want children hanging about. At least the girl wasn't making herself at home.

"Sam, come on. You know what Dad said about being around here."

Sam slid off the couch and followed Maddie out the door. Claudie closed the door after them and although happy they had left, she wondered what exactly Peter had said about her. She looked at the chair. It had to go. Perhaps when the kids were at school would be a better time.

Outside Maddie reminded Sam that their father had said to stay away from Claudie. There was something wrong with her. And it was Chrystal who had brought her into their home.

Across the street the indomitable Mrs. Fowler was feeling a warm glow. That was definitely not an invalid aunt pushing that recliner. That Chrystal hussy was trying to pull a fast one but it would take more than a ticky-tacky bitch like her to fool Ina Mae Fowler. She went in search of her camera; she would be ready next time.

Chrystal looked at the dry-erase board on the side of the refrigerator; it was where she usually wrote down grocery reminders. Today in Maddie's neat printing was written "Word of the Week" and this week's word was *termagant*. Chrystal frowned. She had never heard of that word but didn't feel the need to add a word that was probably only found in books. Whoever used words like that?

She jumped when Peter spoke behind her. "I thought the idea was Mrs. O'Brien was supposed to be representing my frail elderly aunt." Under Chrystal's watchful eye Peter finished rinsing a plate before putting it in the dishwasher. It was part of her campaign for a new dishwasher to have everything clean before going in the old "ratty" dishwasher. She was again being stymied by Peter's natural accommodation. It was going to take an escalation of methods to needle him into the kitchen remodel that was next on her agenda.

"It's true she's not as frail as I'd hoped. I've tried to tell her I can do her shopping and stuff but she keeps popping out. You shouldn't have towed her car back."

"She's popping out again and with a suitcase. The radio has

been going on all morning about a snow advisory. If I get a lot of calls, I want to be pulling paying customers out of ditches—not her. Where the hell does she go?"

"She told me she goes to the library and I know she goes to the health food store—I recognize the bags. I suppose it's a good thing for her. We don't want her brooding in there and going off the deep end again." Chrystal immediately realized her mistake. "Not that I get any sense that she's unbalanced or anything. She's always pretty cheerful when I talk to her."

Peter stared after the departing BMW and then his gaze shifted across the street to Mrs. Fowler's. It looked like Marty was back; there was an old white Ford pick-up that looked like it had crawled out from a rock pile and then a flock of geese had shat on it. If Mrs. Fowler wasn't such a haughty old bitch he would almost feel sorry for her. It must have been quite a blow when Mr. Fowler had sold off most of his family's old homestead and run off with his dental assistant. Mrs. Fowler was left with just a couple of acres, the house, and a decrepit old barn out back. But she retained her pride. A few of the neighbors even tried to help but she was not about to accept pity from the riffraff on what she called ticky-tacky row.

Peter didn't think Marty had been much comfort to her. Of course her son was headed for juvie even before his father ran off. Almost everybody on the road had long ago enclosed their mailboxes with sturdy brick surrounds after Marty took up the sport of mailbox bashing. He graduated to knocking off the outside mirrors of any cars parked on the street. In a small town it was easy to pinpoint the troublemakers, but Marty stood out even in grade school. He rarely hurt people, but he sure did like to break things. He would steal something even if he didn't have a use for it. He took pleasure in watching the victims search in frustration. Sometimes he would put it back. Broken of course. His penchant for hanging around to observe the effects of his misdemeanors was what got him in trouble. He just had to see. Pretty soon he saw the inside of the county jailhouse and Peter hadn't seen him around for a couple of years. By the looks of the pick-up he had not advanced far in life. Maybe it would keep Mrs. Fowler busy and out of their business.

Chapter Six

Marty lay on the old sofa bed staring up at the cobwebby water pipes overhead. He was thinking. He'd been thinking since his little walk the other day. When his mom's nattering had become a near-incitement to matricide he had gone outside to clear his head. His parole officer had drummed into him the importance of walking away when trouble started to brew. He headed out to the old barn set back a few hundred feet from the old farmhouse. He used to play out here when he was a kid; flashlight tag at night in the summers and there was the year they made it a haunted barn and tried to sell tickets. Unfortunately Robin Hargreave had decided to conceal himself in one of the old freezers his grandfather had collected over the years, and if it wasn't for the batteries dying in the boom box they would never have heard his cries for help. It put a damper on the evening and his father and Mr. Hargreave would have had a fistfight if Ina Fowler hadn't turned the water on them. When he got older Marty used the barn for more grown-up pursuits. He lost his virginity with Polly Anne Smithers, the sophomore girl with the senior-level tits. That was the year they both discovered dope. Good times.

He pulled open the old wooden door and stepped into the half-light. It was freezing and kind of spooky; the discarded appliances lined the back and the sepulcher-white tank of farm fertilizer sat in the corner—the only sign that the barn had once been part of an active farm. Marty found the switch and flipped it. The lights contributed meagerly to visibility. He never knew why his grandfather had acquired all the old freezers and refrigerators. His father complained because with the new environmental laws it would cost a bundle to get rid of them with the Freon disposal. So here they sat. He wandered to the back, avoiding the ragged wooden planks covering the old well. Another thing his father complained about—a safety hazard he said—but he never took the time to put a concrete cover over it. Marty found himself looking at the old fertilizer tank: anhydrous ammonia. It looked half full. Then he did a 360 and he began to think.

He was still thinking when his mom screamed down to him to come up and help her with something. He went up and while she was blathering on about the old lady across the street he decided to give Jason a call. Jason was good at putting ideas into action.

Claudie was on the spot. Her car was packed with boxes from her Portland house and she had just finished carrying one into the garage apartment when who should be hovering there volunteering her gap-toothed son to help her? Mrs. Fowler. The son had trailed her out of the house, letting the little black pug escape, and he was standing there eyeing Claudie's BMW and boxes of possessions like he was scoping out where to get the money for his next stash of meth. He had even grabbed a box—her good crystal by the sounds of it. No way did she want him to come inside her apartment or to give Mrs. Fowler any chance to strike up a friendly chat. She was saved by Peter pulling his tow-truck up in front of the house.

Peter ambled over to the little threesome and quickly grasped the situation. Marty had not improved with the passage of time. His hair was thinner and his face had become a wasteland of acne. Peter wasn't naïve enough to think the offer to help was a genuine neighborly gesture. Mrs. Fowler had been trying to poke her nose in the apartment for months and was probably dying to talk Claudie up.

With the hearty manner of a vice-principal at a PTA meeting he reached for the box in Marty's arms. There was a slight hesitation on Marty's part and then he released the box just as Peter put his hands on it. There was a loud tinkle of glass but the box didn't fall.

"Oh man, Teach, you nearly dropped it." Marty laughed and then turned around and went home. Mrs. Fowler hesitated but then followed him. Outmaneuvered and not happy about it.

There were five more boxes but none of them heavy, so he was perplexed what she could have in them. She was unpacking one when he brought the last box in and watched as she unwrapped what was obviously expensive glassware and lined them up in the cupboard.

"Thank you again, Peter. I didn't want that scuddzy son of hers inside my house. Oh Christ, that stupid dog's inside."

Peter reached down and scooped the black pug up and released it outside. It ran back home and started hopping and yapping outside the door until Mrs. Fowler let it in.

"I don't want to pry but what's all this stuff? I thought Chrystal furnished the place with everything you'd need."

Claudie thought hard; she really didn't want to be rude. Peter had left her alone so far and she didn't want to antagonize him.

"Oh she did. It's just that when you get to be my age you kind of like to have your own things around. I have all this stuff back at my Portland place and I thought I'd just bring a few things over to make it feel more like home. You know how it is." She took some old photo albums out of the last box and put them on the coffee table.

Peter shrugged, but when he looked over at the recliner he felt a tinge of what she meant.

She followed his glance and said, "Sam said that was your favorite chair. If you want it back you wouldn't hurt my feelings any."

He sighed, "Nah, Chrystal said it was too big for the room. So you have a home? Portland?"

"Yes."

"We kind of thought you were ah …"

"Homeless? No, I have nice place."

"Then why did you agree to come here?"

"I needed a change of place. Under the circumstances I didn't think it was a good idea to go back to where I was before."

Peter nodded. He knew about unhappy memories. It was one reason he went along with Chrystal's refurnishing plans. The old furniture had a lot of memories spilled on them. Spilling anything on the new furniture would be a capital offense.

"If you find someone who desperately needs a place to live I'd understand."

"No, it's fine." He smiled at Claudie for the first time—a genuine smile.

She thought it was quite a pleasant smile. She wondered, not for the first time, how he had ever become involved with a woman like Chrystal. But people often didn't understand the attractions between other people.

"By the way, Sam wanted me to ask you if you wanted to join us for Thanksgiving dinner next week? He's worried you'll be alone."

Claudie hesitated. She used to love Thanksgiving with friends but it had been a long time. Thanksgiving with strangers made her feel uncomfortable.

"I don't mean to sound like the kids are the only ones who'd like you to come over. Chrystal and I, we'd both like you to come. We have a couple of friends joining us too."

"Thank you, really. But no. I made plans to meet a friend."

After he left, Claudie continued unpacking and she realized that she had brought all this dinnerware but she had no one to ask to dinner. Why in the world did she do this? Well, she was going to have to shop and cook some decent meals for herself. Why the hell not? If she wasn't going to kill herself right away she should enjoy food and wine as much as she could afford.

Across the road Marty had taken a quick bath and retreated downstairs and Mrs. Fowler checked on her pot roast. She hoped the warm meat smell would entice Marty upstairs for a real sit down supper. Most of the time he skulked downstairs, surfacing only to take the rare bath and rummage around in the refrigerator in the middle of the night. Today was one of his sporadic personal hygiene days. She wished that they included cleaning up afterward. In the bathroom she found the faded white underwear with the unmentionable brown skid marks, which she'd thought she would never have to deal with again. And why he insisted on baths instead of showers she didn't know. The bathtub was a grey scuddzy mess.

With a deep sigh she delicately lifted the offending underwear and tossed them down the laundry chute. Immediately she winced; she hoped they didn't land on anything of hers. She would have to go downstairs and sort the laundry. She did Marty's with extra bleach. Getting down to clean the tub was a laborious process. She needed to kneel on a folded towel because of her artificial knee and leaning down to scrub wreaked havoc on her bad back. It took forever to finally pull herself up. If she could only find a decent cleaning woman— one who lived up to her standards. The few that she had hired in the past usually only lasted a month or two before quitting. It was a disgrace. In this economy you would think people would be begging for good employment.

The house was getting to be too much for her. And these old farmhouses never had adequate insulation. The winters were getting colder and colder. She had considered her sister's offer to visit over the holidays but now that Marty was out and at home she was reluctant to leave. Not that Marty couldn't take care of himself; he was a grown man but even she couldn't ignore the uneasy notion that the house might be in sorrier condition if left in his lone hands. She was popped out of her reverie by the sudden blasting of some nasty-sounding rap music downstairs. Pooh started barking and running around the living room and it took some effort to stop grinding her molars and head for the circuit breaker box in the mud porch out back. She went out and flipped the switch for the downstairs outlets. Quiet for the few minutes before Marty trumped upstairs.

"You know, Mom, you should really call an electrician about that circuit breaker. It tripped again." Marty had changed into what were for him dress clothes: semi-clean jeans, a plaid flannel shirt, and a leather jacket. A wash of heavy cologne had followed him up the stairs and supplanted the juicy pot roast smells. He was jingling his truck keys and heading towards the door.

"Aren't you going to stay for supper? The pot roast is almost done and I made an apple pie."

"I'll grab some when I get home. I'm meeting Jason for a few beers." He avoided his mother's anxious look at the word beers and slipped out the door.

She watched as her hopes for a nice family supper dissipated quicker than the cologne fumes. Marty started the truck and pulled away with a thick black cloud of exhaust. A muffler emitted sounds like a pig being chased by the farmer's wife, announcing to the neighborhood that Marty had left the building.

Marty and Jason were finishing their third PBR when Jason's friend Gordon joined them and ordered a pint of Deschutes Black Porter. They would have stepped up to this higher testosterone level of brew if they were assured that Gordon would pick up the tab but they weren't convinced that what they had to offer would interest him enough to pony up. But they needn't have worried. They sparked his interest when they described the isolated barn, the cache of old anhydrous ammonia fertilizer, and the abandoned freezers that still had copious amounts of Freon. Plus the haul of pseudoephedrine that Jason had scored on his last after-hours shopping trip to an eastern Oregon Walgreens. It added the essential ingredient for a home-grown business plan. They began to put together a supply list.

Chapter Seven

Mrs. Boyle's high heels clicked down the busy hospital corridor. She deftly threaded her way between nurses, orderlies, and stray patients before turning into the carpeted suite of administrative offices. As the hospital's head social worker she rated a small but private office. She shut the door behind her and sat down heavily at her cluttered desk. The morning mail had been deposited in a tray on a corner of the desk and without pausing to check her email she scooped up the snail mail and rifled through the envelopes.

Nothing from Claudette O'Brien or her legal firm. Good. Or was it? The old woman could have decided not to pursue a legal claim or she could still be conferring with a law firm. Although Mrs. Boyle was confident that there was no basis for legal action she had reviewed the surveillance tapes and there was no indication that Mrs. O'Brien had been injured by any hospital personnel. That did not necessarily prevent any of the more rapacious law firms from pursuing a spurious claim. The Director of the hospital was keen on her putting the whole issue to rest. Mrs. Boyle had called and left messages several times at the number that Chrystal had given her but there had been no response.

She couldn't decide if a visit might be in order. On one hand it might be the personal touch that would assuage a disgruntled patient. On the other hand it might provoke the opposite reaction; it might look like the hospital was nervous and open to exploitation. She needed to show her boss that she was doing something though. She picked up a golf-ball-sized crystal that had been anchoring some papers and gazed into its clear depths. Usually this helped her focus but not today. It was like her aura was muddied. She would have to work on it this weekend.

She was pulled away from this indecisive deliberation by the rising sounds of voices in the reception area. Now what? She opened her door and looked out to where the receptionist was standing as if blocking another woman from proceeding to the offices. The woman was protesting her exclusion with increasing volume and liberal cuss words. This was not to be tolerated, Mrs. Boyle thought as she marched down to the beleaguered receptionist.

"What is going on here? Gretchen, who is this person?" Mrs. Boyle addressed her comment to the receptionist but turned a most severe and humorless stare at the intruder.

"I'm so sorry Mrs. Boyle. This is Corrine Bales. She's a patient and she's demanding to speak with the Director."

Mrs. Bales, who was dressed in a dark if seriously dated suit, was returning Mrs. Boyle's glare ounce for ounce. The outrage of others at her behavior barely pricked her consciousness.

"I must see the person in charge immediately. There is something seriously amiss at this hospital and there could be dire consequences if someone doesn't listen to me." Corrine delivered this with a gravity that, combined with her somber appearance, gave Mrs. Boyle pause.

"The Director is in Seattle at a conference."

"Well someone must be the fuck in charge. The monkeys aren't running the hen house." Corrine's mixed metaphors would be of considerable amusement if they weren't always delivered with such liberal use of invective and venom.

"I'm Mrs. Boyle. If you'd like to come back to my office perhaps I can be of help." Mrs. Boyle smiled tightly and with a sweep of her arm indicated her open office door. When Corrine headed towards the office Mrs. Boyle whispered to the hapless Gretchen, "Find out where in the hospital this woman comes from and get one of her doctors here immediately. With sedatives."

In her office Mrs. Boyle found Corrine perched on the chair in front of her desk looking like a small baleful crow. She smiled at her own little pun.

"So what is your position here?" Corrine accompanied her acerbic demand with a flinty scrutiny of Mrs. Boyle's name plaque on her desk.

Mrs. Boyle settled into her chair, taking her time to answer. "I am the senior administrator in social services. Why don't you tell me about the dire problem you think the hospital needs to know about."

Corrine squinted at Mrs. Boyle, trying to detect if there was any signs of patronizing. Satisfied at this juncture that she had reached someone important enough to listen to her, she started her tale.

And Mrs. Boyle tried mightily to follow the meandering narrative and maintain a straight face. The woman was obviously unhinged; she hoped there was help on the way. The phone rang, causing Mrs. Boyle to jump and Corrine to glower as she answered it.

"Mrs. Boyle, Corrine Bales was just released. She's the one who came out of a coma after a month, you remember? Her doctor has been looking all over the hospital for her. She's arranged transportation to take her home. She's on her way with one of the nurses."

Mrs. Boyle hung up and nodded for Corrine to proceed. Of course, the old bat lived in Sisters. Mrs. Boyle had seen her occasionally on the weekends when she went in to work in her little shop. Amazingly they had never really crossed paths until now. On the weekends Mrs. Boyle was a completely different person; her real self emerged. It was more a reflection of her spiritual being—one where her soul communed with the mystery of the cosmos. She was brought back to the here and now when Corrine snapped at her.

"Why aren't you taking notes? Fucking A, don't you people understand that a woman's life is in danger? A murder most foul was being plotted in my room and you folks just let them walk out of the hospital, and it's me who you're giving a raft of shit."

"Corrine, no one is giving you a raft of … of … crap. I understand that you've been through a horrible ordeal. Often people who have been in comas experience confusion when they first come out."

"Jesus S. Christ, I am not confused. I'm as fucking sane as you, no, more than you. I've had two weeks to try to sort out what I heard and I know that there were two women in my room and they were plotting to kill a woman because of a garage." Corrine banged her hand on the desk sending a small pile of files slanting towards the floor.

"A garage?" Mrs. Boyle nudged the files back before they sailed to the carpet. This time she knew that the amusement in her voice betrayed her.

"You think that's funny don't you? People have been killed for less. My uncle Floyd was shot because of a goat." Before the story of the goat could unfold, the door opened and a

middle-aged woman stood there, looking relieved yet dis-
mayed at her agitated patient.

"Oh look, your doctor has finally found you. And the
nurse would like to give you a little something to settle your
nerves." Mrs. Boyle stood as the nurse handed Corrine a small
paper cup of water and a two-mg tablet of Ativan.

Corrine was torn. She wanted to fling the water into the
silly bitch's face but she dearly loved her Ativan. She was
quite addicted to it now. Well, none of these ninnies were
going to be any help anyway so she popped the pill and drank
part of the water. She was going to have to find another way
to search for the plotters. She stood and set the paper cup
down next to the pile of files. She looked up at Mrs. Boyle
and damn if the bitch didn't look like she was smirking in
triumph. With a slight spasm of her hand she sent the files,
with paper cup and water tumbling after, down to the floor.
With a small "oops" she followed the nurse out of the office.

Gretchen stood uncertainly in Mrs. Boyle's doorway. "Are
you all right?"

"I'm fine, Gretchen. You did well. It was quite the excitement for the day." Mrs. Boyle had picked up the files and was
shaking the water from them.

"What was it all about, the murder plot?"

"Nothing, she's just confused from the coma dreams." Mrs.
Boyle sat back at her desk and tried to collect her thoughts.

Ha! Murderous goats. Garages provoking a most foul murder plot. Who would have known? On the weekends when

she worked with people who were seeking answers to their spiritual difficulties, she had listened to a lot of strange stories. Corrine's was definitely one of the strangest. She had a very bad aura. Mrs. Boyle rarely said that about people but Corrine was definitely a reddish brown. Angry and troubled.

She sorted through her thoughts. Where was she when the hysterical Corrine Bales interrupted her? Ah, Mrs. O'Brien. She pictured Claudie sitting in that wheelchair, reeking of sour wine and that smug little tart in the flashy clothes standing beside her. And there, behind them was another patient in a bed. Mrs. Boyle frowned and picked up the phone.

"Gretchen, what room was Corrine Bales in when she came out of her coma?"

Gretchen referred to a piece of paper on her desk, "302."

Mrs. Boyle hung up without thanking her. Fuck. The same room as Mrs. Fucking Claudette O'Brien. Now what?

"Are you sure you don't mind, Claudie? It's just that I forgot it was an in-service day at school and the kids would be at home. The refrigerator is completely empty." Chrystal stood in the kitchen doorway putting her coat on over her yoga clothes. Claudie noticed that her makeup was a little elaborate for a yoga class. The woman probably never left the house without a perfectly applied face.

"It's fine. I needed to go to the store anyway. Do you have

a list?" Claudie strove to keep any sign of annoyance out of her voice.

"Yes, it's there on the counter with the money. Maddie can help. Just don't let them get any junk food, sodas, sugary stuff, or red meat." Chrystal retreated to the front hall and screamed up the stairs, "Maddie, get down here. Maddie!" There was no response. Chrystal checked her phone for the time and then began texting.

"Sometimes it's easier to get her attention with a text. If she isn't down in five you might have to go up. You'll recognize her door by the 'Keep Out' signs." Chrystal tucked her phone in her coat pocket and opened the door.

"You forgot your mat." Claudie pointed at the roll by the door.

Chrystal looked at the foam roll blankly and then with a grin grabbed it and escaped. Claudie looked up the stairs and then went back to the kitchen to review the list. It was a depressing catalog of gluten free and soy protein products with a number of healthy vegetables, none of which were known to entice teenagers to the merits of good nutrition. The contents of the refrigerator were indeed sparse. She was examining the dry-erase board with the word of the week *harridan* when Maddie wandered in. She looked grumpy and rumpled in red flannel pajamas and said not a word as Claudie completed her inspection.

"Spaghetti?"

"What about it?"

"Do you and Sam like it?"

"As long as Chrystal doesn't make it. Sam likes Spaghetti-Os."

"That's not spaghetti. Real spaghetti is easy enough to make. I can show you."

"Why?" Maddie sat on a stool and rested her head on the kitchen island counter.

"If you don't like Chrystal's cooking, then I suggest you learn to cook defensively."

Maddie just shrugged noncommittally. Sam poked his head in and then pulled out the stool next to Maddie and sat.

"Go upstairs and change while Sam and I work up a list and then we can all go to the store."

"I'll just put my coat on over this."

"In my youth pajamas were nightwear never to be worn outside unless for a mad dash for the newspaper. If you want me to help you, then you need to go put on some jeans and a sweater, non-negotiable."

"Then go without me." Maddie started to slide off the stool.

"Nope. I'm not your servant but I agreed to help. If you want food then you need to come along and lend a hand."

"Please Maddie. I'm hungry." Sam put on the puppy-dog thing he did with his eyes.

Maddie grimaced at him and then reluctantly headed for the stairs.

"Put some real shoes on too. No bedroom slippers outside the house." Claudie called out to her retreating back.

"You're pushing it, Coly."

Claudie cast a quizzical eye at Sam, "Collie?" Sam just rolled his shoulders in a shrug and avoided her look. Claudie let it drop. She sat next to Sam and started a list with real food.

Chrystal was deeply immersed in exploring her seven Chakras through Tantric yoga. Currently this involved Ray attempting to release her blocked energy flow by stimulating her G-spot. At least he said it was her G-spot. So far she had not noticed any difference in the duration of her orgasms. He had told her that once he released all her blocked Chakras, and the G-spot seemed key to this, then she would be able to sustain orgasms for up to nine hours. Jesus, who the hell had time for that? It made her shudder.

Ray took that as an encouraging sign. He indicated the next position and she diligently extended her legs to the ceiling. As they progressed she inhaled as deeply as she could and then began the "aaaaaah" on the exhale. This was supposed to link her Chakras and intensify the orgasm. She hadn't noticed a difference there either. Ray came to a shuddering conclusion and then remained inside and on top of her. She found this rather annoying; he was heavy and sweaty and she knew from experience that he had remarkable powers of recovery. She needed to shower and dress for her shift and did not have any more time to devote to releasing her energy flows. Ray was unwavering in his devotion to her fields of energy. He said her Chakras were excessively contaminated and needed the constant application of energy therapies. He was tireless in his efforts to free her of these negative forces.

When they were not working on her poor Chakras, Ray spent their time espousing his theories about how the marriage of science, biology, and quantum physics had begun to reveal to man the wisdom of the ancients. It was very confusing to Chrystal. She had never been very good at science in school. She was satisfied letting it all remain a mystery. What she wanted was some progress on financing the spiritual retreat. So far Ray had made only marginal headway in locating suitable harmonic sites. She had seen no drawings or designs for the holistic center.

She managed to extricate herself from under him before his energies were flowing again. As she showered and dressed she wondered how she could nudge him in more down-to-earth pursuits. Her Chakras could wait; her mother was coming to visit at Christmas and she wanted to have some concrete plans to show her. Maybe she could lay off a few cruises and contribute to the cause.

When she went back into the bedroom Ray was leaning against the headboard drawing on a large joint. That was another thing that was holding the show up. If it weren't for his new Porsche and the expensive hotel suite she would think he was just another stoner with big smoke-induced pie-in-the-sky plans. She gave him a little wave from the door and left.

It had been a long day that had oozed into the early evening when he got a call about a Kia in a ditch. It was a college kid who hadn't bothered to put chains on before going to play in the snow. It was a cold wet job getting him out and of course the kid was too poor to think about tipping. All Peter wanted to do was to get home and change into warm dry clothes. With some luck Chrystal might be home early from work.

The house had an odd smell. Peter stood in the entryway slowly taking off his coat and boots, trying to identify the odor. It was food, and he followed the scent into the kitchen. The kitchen was empty and the sink and counters clean, though there was a note on the island.

> *Dad, there's real food in the fridge.*
> *Love, Maddie*

Beneath Maddie's signature Sam had added, '*Claudie is really a good cook! It's better than spagetios!*'

Peter opened the refrigerator and pulled out the leftovers. Not being a fan of Spaghetti-Os, Sam's endorsement was less than sterling, but the smell lingering in the kitchen was encouraging. He glanced at the clock; it was after ten and a little late for a heavy meal but after microwaving a dish of fragrant pasta and sauce he had to agree with Sam—way better than Spaghetti-Os.

He was exhausted; hooking up a car in an icy ditch to tow it would do that to you. His body cried out for bed but Chrystal's car was not in the drive and he thought he would watch some TV until she got home. They hadn't had a chance to talk for a while.

He woke during the transition from *The Daily Show* to *The Stephen Colbert Report* and turned the TV off. He checked out the window but still no car. Upstairs he stripped to his tee shirt and boxers and was about to climb in his side when he noticed a book on Chrystal's bedside stand. He picked it up, *The Delta of Venus* by Anais Nin. Hmmm. He thought Nora Roberts was more her style. Maybe he had something to look forward to.

Their sex life had dwindled to non-existent. They were both too tired. Once again he hoped that the next legislature would find more money for schools. He missed his job. The kids and the teachers could be pains but they were still more interesting than stranded tourists or numbnut skiers who couldn't put their chains on properly. And if he went back to teaching or as vice-principal, Chrystal could quit her job at Six Firs. He had not anticipated how many hours she would be expected to put in. He rolled over to his side and turned out the light. He was asleep long before Chrystal rolled in.

Chapter Eight

"Okay, the turkey's in the oven and the timer is on. The side dishes are in the fridge and I put notes on them telling you how long to microwave them. Any questions?" Chrystal was slipping her feet into boots and clutching a plastic bag with her high heels.

"Yes, why in the world did you not know you had to work this shift at Six Firs?" Peter's voice was measured. He was trying to control his aggravation but he wasn't sure who to be angry at.

"I wasn't supposed to be working is why. Beth Ann called in sick although I think it has more to do with the new boyfriend. She told me he was going skiing in Washington over the holidays. I bet you anything she's gone with him." She stood impatiently by the door.

He didn't often see her when she left for work and she looked radiant. Her makeup was perfect and the sleek dress beneath the coat was sexy as all get out. It almost made him more furious that all that gorgeousness was leaving to be bestowed on someone else. And she didn't even seem to mind that she was deserting the family on Thanksgiving.

"I don't give a fu—damn about Beth Ann and her stupid boyfriend. Why'd they call you in? Don't they know you have a family? What kind of people do you work for? I should call that manager and remind him that Thanksgiving is a time to spend at home with family. You used to say that my—our family was the most important thing in your life. What happened to that? Don't we count anymore?"

"Oh, don't be so dramatic. We need this paycheck, remember?" It was the cruelest thing Chrystal could say to prevent him from calling and finding out that her services were not in fact needed on this holiday.

Peter, his faced flushed with anger, turned around and went into the kitchen. He hated it that Chrystal's jibes hurt but they did. The kids were upstairs in their rooms; he knew they wouldn't miss Chrystal, but he still hoped that if only they could have enough good times together that they would finally become the family he wished for. He realized he was the only one in the house who still dreamed about them becoming a family. Well, maybe Sam too.

He called up the stairs, "Maddie. Maddie, could you come down here?"

Maddie, still clad in her flannel PJs, came down and found her father digging around in the bureau with all the table-cloths and stuff.

"Could you put this on the table and get it set for dinner? Chrystal's been called into work and we need to finish getting things ready." He tossed her a white linen tablecloth and began counting cloth napkins. Did they even have four that matched anymore?

Maddie didn't even try to mask her happiness that Chrystal wasn't going to be with them. They both heard the front door slam shut and the car starting up in the driveway. Peter glanced out the window and watched her go. He noticed that Claudie's car was missing.

"Okay, TJ is coming at two o'clock. Chrystal set the timer for when the turkey comes out. We're good till then."

Maddie went into the kitchen, looked at the timer, opened the oven, and then stood open mouthed as the heat surged out.

"Dad!" Her voice had that panic quality that sends shivers down a parent's spine. Peter was in the kitchen in a second.

"That's not a turkey! Dad! She put a fake turkey in there. She's not even going to be here and she's ruining Thanksgiving." Maddie's shrill voice had alerted Sam to the disaster. He stood behind his dad and looked at the thing in the oven.

Peter shut the oven on the pan containing the Tofurky. Even he thought it was a dispiriting sight.

"Okay, we can fix this. I can go to the store and get a turkey. Dinner will just be a little later." He started for the front door and was putting on his coat when he stopped; the store was closed and even if it were open the only turkeys they had would be frozen. Maddie and Sam followed him to the door with expectant eyes but they could see the sign of defeat in his eyes.

"You let her ruin it. She ruins everything. Why did you marry such a stupid bitch?"

"Maddie."

"I don't care. You eat the rubber turkey, I'm not." Maddie turned and raced upstairs, her bedroom door slamming reverberated downstairs. Sam stood frozen in place. Peter sat at the table and tried to figure out how he could fix this. He was coming up with nothing.

"It's okay, Dad. I can eat the Tofurky. It won't be that bad." Sam sat down beside his father with a serious face. "Too bad Claudie isn't here. She'd fix it."

"I don't even know if Julia Child could fix this, buddy."

"Who's Julia Child?"

"Someone who handled cooking disasters with aplomb."

"A plum?"

"Sorry kiddo. I mean she knew how to roll with the punches."

Peter got up and finished setting the table. Maddie came

down and without saying a word picked up the napkins and started playing with different ways to fold them. Chrystal's laptop was sitting on the tiny desk and she opened it and started Googling different ways to fold cloth napkins. She selected one pattern and enlisted Sam in helping her. When they were finished she silently went back upstairs with the laptop under her arm.

Claudie pulled into Black Butte Ranch and drove to the restaurant parking area. It was a spur of the moment decision. She had to get away after telling Peter that she had plans. Going out to a fancy restaurant on a holiday was one of her least favorite things but it was the price she paid for lying. The restaurant reception area was packed and she had to weave to the front to place her name on the list. Without a reservation it was going to be a long wait. The people milling about were all dressed in their Sunday best and she realized that she had seriously underdressed for the restaurant. Well screw them. She went into the cocktail lounge. It was also crowded but the bar was empty and she sat down on a stool. At least the wine list was good.

She started with a glass of champagne—the first since her little 'accident'. It was fruity without being sweet and she started to watch people as they drifted in and out of the bar. Most of them were older adults although a few groups had children. The children looked bored because it appeared that mobile devices were forbidden. She could hear a sharp peal of laughter out in the reception area that reminded her a little of Chrystal's brittle laugh. She looked out and could see the back of a blonde woman in a tiny snug black dress. She was talking to another woman whose face was composed into a polite plane of indifference. A tall man with grey hair had his arm around the waist of the blonde woman. He leaned slightly and said something in her ear and, when she turned slightly to hear him better, Claudie realized with a start that it was in fact Chrystal.

Claudie couldn't see Peter or the kids and she suddenly grasped that she wasn't going to. For whatever reason Chrystal was here with other people, with another man, and her family was at home. How Chrystal had pulled that off didn't concern Claudie as much as how she was going to avoid being seen. She was watching a secret unfold and she didn't want Chrystal to know she was caught out in her lie.

Claudie took one last swallow of the champagne and waited till Chrystal and her friends moved away from the entryway. She laid money on the bar and walked to the door. Chrystal's group must have been shown to a table so she cut left and went out to the parking lot. She breathed in the cold air and thought about what food she had at home. At least now she didn't have to eat bland overcooked turkey.

She parked her car in time to see a man go into Peter's house. At least it appeared that they were celebrating even without dear Chrystal. Inside she opened the refrigerator and took stock. In a flash she knew what she could whip up: the true Thanksgiving dish according to that expert, Calvin Trillin. Spaghetti Carbonara.

She was grating the Parmigiano-Reggiano when there was a tap on the door. Sam stood in the cold wearing a dress shirt and his hair slicked back.

"Do you want to come over? We're having rubber turkey, which I bet you've never had before. Maddie's had a hissy fit but she's okay now and Dad and his friends are drinking Scotch and wanted to know if you'd like come over for a drink." Sam looked up at her eagerly like rubber turkey would indeed be something to entice somebody. Claudie couldn't help but laugh.

"Sure. I can come by for a drink. Let me grab my wine. I don't much care for scotch. It tastes like rubbing alcohol that's been filtered through charcoal briquettes."

Sam shrugged. He wasn't offended by the aspersion on scotch.

Next door she found Peter and Maddie in the kitchen. "Sam's invited me over for a drink and some rubber turkey. I couldn't resist."

"We've had a bit of a crisis. Chrystal had to go into work and the kids are upset."

"Chrystal bought a fake turkey. It's not a real turkey—it's tofu and some brown shit."

"Maddie!"

"It's true. I read the label."

"It is? I have to see this." Claudie opened the oven door and looked briefly at the dull brown tube of soybean product. She hastily closed the oven. And now she had a choice. Leave this dysfunctional family to sort it out on their own, Peter was a grown-up, but the kids were having a tough time. All the while Chrystal was living it up at Black Butte with her new lover.

"I can't help on the turkey front but if you're flexible I might be able to help with something more appetizing. Tell me, Peter. Have you ever told Maddie and Sam the true story about the first Thanksgiving?"

Peter looked puzzled and shook his head.

"Maddie, where's your laptop? I want you to look up Calvin Trillin and his story about the original Thanksgiving feast."

After twenty minutes Claudie had explained how the legend of the first Thanksgiving had been misinterpreted and that the Native Americans had not been thrilled with the Pilgrims' overcooked turkey and vegetables. They preferred the legendary meal provided by the 'big Italian fellow' who had dropped by a century or so before. They still told stories about that wonderful dish of Spaghetti Carbonara. As far as they were concerned, the Pilgrims were just a bunch of turkeys.[1]

Fortunately Claudie had enough of the main ingredients to make a decent batch big enough for five. She served the

1   Calvin Trillin "Third Helpings"

kale and beet slaw and mashed cauliflower with chia seeds that Chrystal had made but they were later returned to the refrigerator mostly intact. Chrystal had also made a low-fat pumpkin pie sweetened only with molasses but fortunately TJ had brought over an apple pie from the Sisters Bakery. Together with the Tofurky, Chrystal would be able to have a complete Thanksgiving dinner for days to come. On the dry-erase board the word of the week was *virago*.

Chrystal had justified her decampment from the family home with the knowledge that A, she wouldn't be missed by the kids and B, she was answering to a higher calling. Vis-à-vis her new spiritual mentor. Ray had been quite depressed the last week or so. His plans for creating an otherworldly retreat for souls seeking a transcendent experience outside the bounds of established religions or sects had hit an unfortunate snag. Lack of money and lack of political clout to persuade the county planning commission to make just one tiny zoning adjustment had stalled his plans. From her own experience she knew how pig-headed the county planning office could be.

She had taken Ray to the Thanksgiving Dinner at Black Butte Ranch. MJ, her boss at High Vista Realty, had mentioned that she was taking some of her newly single clients there. Chrystal was hoping that during the course of the dinner some of MJ's rich friends might stop by the table and she could introduce Ray. Some of these people must be in a position to help politically or financially. What was the point of having connections with people with money if you couldn't help relieve them of some of it? Chrystal knew this was a somewhat cynical attitude but Ray assured her that the pursuit of spiritual truth was a higher mission that justified unconventional methods. The rich were often burdened with the toxic residue of their secular quest for the gaudy baubles of their world. Anything Ray could do to help these people find a way to free themselves of this waste and attain enlightenment was all to the moral good of the planet.

Back at the Walker table, after the kids deserted the adults, TJ began telling them about his father who had been on track to make tenure at the University of Wisconsin. Apparently seducing the teenage daughter of the English department's dean was considered a transgression worthy of banishment. TJ was mostly worried that his mother might ship him west and there was no way he was going to let his father move in with him. He could bunk with his sister Corrine. They deserved each other.

Peter raised his glass. "I want to toast Claudie. You have single-handedly rescued us from a dismal meal. I can't thank you enough and I'm sure the kids will agree."

TJ raised his beer and drank. "And I want to thank you, Peter. I was afraid that I'd have to spend Thanksgiving with my ditsy aunt Corrine. It's hard when your only nearby relative is a crazy aunt who drinks too much and rants about the government conspiracy to control the weather. Thank you for inviting me to spend time around a normal family."

"I'm not too sure how normal we are. But you're welcome."

Claudie suppressed a cough at the description of "normal family" and then said, "You left your poor aunt alone on Thanksgiving?"

"I checked on her earlier and she was already into the vodka. She had some deli turkey and was fixated on her computer looking through county permit records. I have no idea what she's going on about now and I want to keep it that way. She was never fond of me anyway so I don't feel too guilty."

"I guess everyone has one or two horror stories from the holidays."

"God, yes." Claudie shook her head and smiled.

"Don't leave it at that, Claudie. You know our dark secrets. Tell us one of yours." TJ didn't see the worried look that Peter flashed Claudie.

Claudie poured another glass of wine and thought for a moment. "Well there was the year of the flying turkey." The men waited expectantly.

"I was cutting the pie for our company and my husband wanders in with the platter with the half-eaten turkey carcass. He wants to know what to do with it. All the counters are covered with dishes and I'm irritated because he hadn't lifted a finger to help with the dinner. He had hit the scotch pretty heavy before dinner and then downed a bottle of pinot with the meal. I was very pissed at him. So I make a crack that if he can't be bothered to help cover it and put it in the refrigerator then he could just chuck the damned bird over the back fence for the coyotes. We lived out in the woods then. I go back to dishing up the pie. I thought he'd find some place to set it down and go back to our guests. A few minutes later I hear the back door slam and he sails in, hands me the empty platter, and goes back to our friends. That man never did a single thing I asked him to except that once. And it was an organic free-range turkey to boot. My friends, who usually left with baggies of turkey, were incredulous. He didn't even remember it in the morning. He said I made it up. Trust me, I didn't have to make up shit about him. He was like crazy Corrine, a continual fount of misdeeds."

TJ looked over to Peter expectantly, "Come on, Peter. I know this Thanksgiving doesn't come anywhere near the one about your mother and the cats and the stove."

"Oh God, no. It took me years before I could eat turkey again." Peter was laughing but he had an embarrassed flush to his face.

"Grandma didn't bake a cat for Thanksgiving did she?" Sam was in the doorway with a look of panic on his face.

"No, no. Do you need some pie?"

Sam nodded but the worry was not draining from his face. He would have to ask Maddie.

Claudie leaned towards TJ while Peter dished up pie for everyone. "Okay, you can't leave it there. What did she do with the cat?"

"It's what the cat did to her. She had about six cats then; it was after Peter's father died and she just started to let things go. They went over for Thanksgiving dinner and when they walked in, there was this God-awful smell. Seemed one of the cats had been peeing on top of the gas stove. She'd cleaned up the top but not where it leaked into the oven. When she turned on the oven the smell just swamped the house. She smoked and she couldn't smell it. Peter said it was so bad it stung his eyes."

Peter returned to the table and set the pie plates down. All eyes were on him to finish the story.

"What did you do?"

"I poured her another rum and coke, a stiff one, and then turned the oven up from 350 to 500 degrees. It only took about twenty minutes for smoke to come billowing out and we turned the oven off and went into town for dinner. She never knew what happened."

They were all laughing so hard they hardly noticed the kids back in the doorway; Sam's face still a model of worry. Maddie assumed it was another stupid adult joke and went back upstairs to the laptop. She was halfway through reading some very juicy emails, not all of which she understood. But she knew enough to know they weren't between her father and Chrystal. Chrystal had someone on the side and now she just had to figure out whom. Someone and their ridiculous white couch could soon be history.

"That was some turkey, Mrs. Fowler. I really appreciate you inviting us to join you and Marty for Thanksgiving." Gordon mopped up the last of the gravy with a Pillsbury dinner roll and rested a contented gaze on Mrs. Fowler who endeavored to bask in his appreciation. It was hard. Marty and his friends Jason and Gordon had hoovered up the meal so fast that she still had nearly a full plate of food. In fact they were nearly finished before she had sat down.

On reflection she wondered if they ate so fast because they had all been in state sponsored detention or because they simply skipped chewing their food and swallowed it whole. If she calculated it she figured that she had put in over an hour of cooking for every minute they spent swallowing—a somewhat lousy return on investment. Of course the less time watching Gordon cram mashed potatoes in like they were on a conveyor belt the better. What little chewing she observed was of the open-mouth variety.

"Yeah, that was some stupendous chow." Jason said around his finger, which was probing deeply for a piece of turkey lodged between his back molars. Truth be told, Mrs. Fowler had cooked the turkey beyond the recommended tempera-ture, mindful of the latest super salmonella scare and determined to thwart the world of evil bacteria that was ever evolving to destroy the good people of America. The turkey breast was tougher than sun baked horseshit.

"I've got some nice apple pie for dessert. Do you boys want it with ice cream or some Cool Whip?"

"Gee, Mom, that sounds great but I'm bursting. We're going to take a little walk to work up an appetite for dessert. You leave the dishes and we'll clean up later."

Marty stood and with several eye rolls got the other two up and heading out the back door. Mrs. Fowler surveyed the table and with a sigh finished eating her Thanksgiving dinner, which was her first with her son in nearly a decade. She felt a soft warm body plop on her feet and she looked down. Pooh had come out of the back bedroom and was taking his usual dinner roost.

Out back the three men crunched through the thin layer of snow to the barn and entered the cold dark interior. Marty flipped the overhead light and led them over to the ammonia tank.

"How old do you think it is?" Jason tapped the plastic tank with his boot.

"Not sure. My grandfather stopped farming sometime in the '90s. He was, boy, maybe eighty-eight or so. Keeled over from a heart attack inspecting a sow over at the neighbor's pig farm. Good thing the other farmer always carried a ball bat when he went into the pigpen. As it was he almost didn't get all of grandpa out of there. I guess the pig ate his boot."

The two friends looked at Marty like he was shitting them but it was too colorful a story for Marty's limited imagination so they just nodded, not knowing what to say. In the brief silence there was a sharp crack and Gordon looked down at the wooden plank he was standing on. There seemed to be a little give to it.

"What's this?"

"Oh, shit dude, you might want to get off that. There's an old well down there."

Gordon gingerly stepped off the wooden planks. "What's it doing in the barn?"

"Fuck if I know. He had cows in here; that's all I remember."

Jason was over looking at the back of the old freezers.

"What about the Freon? Do you know how to drain it out of these things?"

"I Googled it. It's a little tricky but doable. I'll need some special equipment. Do you got the list?"

Gordon pulled a piece of paper out of his back pocket and they started going over it and planning the layout. When it got too cold for them they trooped back to the house and apple pie. After the pie, which took them less than sixty seconds to consume, they headed out.

Mrs. Fowler looked at the dirty dishes that Marty had promised to clean. Not that she would have let them clean. She shuddered to think of the less than sanitary results that they would have produced. None of them, not one of them, had washed their hands before dinner. She started to run water in the sink and stood looking out the window to the backyard. She noticed the tracks of the three men leading directly to the barn. Huh, probably went out there to smoke. Cigarettes she hoped. Marty was still on probation and they could test him any time for drugs. She was going to have to keep a close eye on him. She wasn't too sure that those two friends were a good influence on him. All his life he kept getting involved with these shady characters; if they would only leave him alone she knew he would straighten out his life, get a job, and maybe even get a wife. Well, not a wife for a while.

"Morning, son."

"Dad." TJ stood in the doorway to his aunt Corrine's house looking at his father. Frank had three-day stubble on his chin that was mostly grey, though his head was still covered with thick brown hair that was a little long.

"Come to visit or gloat? Did your mom send you?" Frank's eyes squinted a little into the bright outdoor light and it gave him a slightly paranoid look. He hadn't stepped back from the door yet to let TJ inside.

"No and no. I came to give Aunt Corrine a drive to the beauty parlor. I didn't know you were here."

"Typical of your mother not to tell you."

"Why? Did you lose my phone number? And are you going to let me in?"

Frank stood back from the door and yelled back into the house to Corrine.

"Your chauffeur to the beauty salon is here, Madam." He walked back to the kitchen and TJ followed him.

"So how goes the police job? Quelled any riots lately?" Frank poured a cup of coffee and sat at the vinyl-covered table.

"We're in short supply of riots in Jefferson County, Dad. You thinking about starting some? Isn't that what you majored in at college? Student agitation? Freedom to the people."

"Damn right."

"Horseshit." Corrine came into the kitchen and started to go through her purse. "Your dad got tear gassed in college once. *By accident.* He walked into the student lounge for a Coke just as someone set off some crappy homemade tear gas bomb. He's been embellishing that for forty years. Have you seen my car keys?"

"No need, Aunt Corrine. I'm here to take you to Liz's and then afterwards we can stop for lunch if you like."

"Jesus S. Christ. I'm not an invalid. Why the hell hasn't that doctor cleared me to drive yet?" She was still digging in her purse and had yet to look up at either man.

"I'm sure when you see him next week he'll release you. In the meantime I'm yours for the asking." TJ immediately regretted that statement. He glanced at his father who was grinning at him. "Of course now that Dad is here I'm sure he'll be happy to take you wherever you need to go." He grinned back at his father.

"Good. 'Cuz one of you is going to have to take me by a couple of places I need to look at."

"What are you looking for, Corrine?" Frank picked up a sheet of paper she had placed by her purse.

"Never you mind, busybody. Why don't you get cleaned up and go look for a job? I'm not supporting you, you know. If your wife kicked you out it's not my job to take care of you."

"Corrine, I just got here. Let a man have a minute to gather his thoughts."

"Thoughts don't buy groceries. Come on, TJ." She headed for the front door and then stopped, looking out at TJ's truck. "Damn, I thought I'd get to ride in your police car."

"I'm not allowed to use the deputy sheriff's car for personal use, Aunt Corrine."

TJ helped her into the passenger side of the truck and they drove away. Inside Frank picked up the phone and dialed Marion, his wife. The phone rang and eventually went to voicemail. She must have gotten wise to him using Corrine's phone. He left another message that he knew would be deleted as soon as she heard his voice. Boy, that woman held a grudge. He went into the bathroom, which was as pink and old fashioned as fuzzy slippers.

Corrine lived a few blocks south of Main Street and after cleaning up he headed towards the cowboy burger joint he'd noticed last night when he drove in. It was closed; it was still only ten thirty so he wandered down the street and into a small bookstore.

It was a cool old-fashioned bookstore, slightly musty smelling with old wood floors and he loved it immediately. All those years of working in the English Departments of various colleges with all the infighting that academia involved had made him nostalgic for a life of quiet contemplation. Surrounded by books and no people sounded like nirvana. He went first to the aisle with literary novels and was methodically reviewing the selection when a man slightly older than himself limped out of the back and stood behind the counter.

"If there's anything you need, let me know."

"Just browsing right now. You work here or do you own the store?"

"Both. Not enough business in the off season to hire any help."

"Damn. I'm staying in town with my sister and I wouldn't mind a little bit of work." Frank stooped down to eye the titles on the lower shelves.

"Oh really. Who's your sister?"

"Corrine Bales."

There was a short silence and Frank looked up at the bookstore owner. "Don't worry. There's usually just one sibling in our family that comes out a little daffy. Corrine is considered to be one of the more, shall I say, unique siblings in a few generations. Once I figured out that my son TJ had not inherited the family peculiarity I told my wife we should just stop."

The man laughed. "Corrine is a force of nature, that's for sure. So TJ is your son? He's a good guy. He comes in here a couple times a month."

"TJ? That's amazing. His mother and I weren't sure he'd even make it out of high school."

"People change. There's not a lot to do in this town."

Frank brought a copy of a Hilary Mantel book to the counter. "If you ever need someone to help you in the store let me know. I'd love to work in a place like this. My name's Frank by the way."

"Nathan. I'll think about it, Frank. I have some knee surgery coming up. I was thinking of closing the store but I'll keep you in mind."

"Fantastic."

TJ parked his car on Oak Street and walked Corrine towards Liz's Cut-n-Go. He almost lost her when she veered towards Sonia's Psychic Reading Parlor. Fortunately Sonia only worked on the weekends in the off-season. He deposited Corrine safely at Liz's. He had an hour and a half before he had to pick her up. Time to do a little Christmas shopping and then he thought he would take her for fish and chips at Hank's on Main Street. He wasn't sure what she had planned but he wasn't interested in getting involved in one of her paranoid plots. His plan was to ply her with a couple of gin and tonics at lunch to mellow her out and take her back home and let his father deal with her.

Mrs. Fowler bent to pick up the brown turds by the porch. Lord, her back hurt. She had let them go when the weather was so cold and now the snow around the front and back door was littered with little tootsie roll piles. She finished the cleanup in the front and walked around to the back door area. She heard footsteps crunching behind her and turned; Jason was coming towards her carrying a large box. With a cheerful hello he passed her and went into the barn.

Marty and the boys were trying to put a band together and spent most of their days in the drafty old barn. The electrical bill had already started to spike up because of the space heaters they had on. Still, she was thankful that they weren't downstairs. From what she could hear blaring out of the barn, their music could stand a lot of work. Of course the popular music nowadays was all pretty much an affront on the ears and central nervous system.

She finished picking up after Pooh and dumped the sack in the garbage. Inside she started a fresh pot of coffee and tidied the kitchen. Marty had made sandwiches for him and the boys, and of course left the mayo, mustard, and bread out. It seemed her days were spent cleaning up after and shopping for Marty and now his friends. She frankly wanted to run away from home. She should call her sister in Mesa and drive down there for a couple of weeks. Vivien was having a hard time of it since Roger had converted to Catholicism when he found out he had the cancer. They hadn't always gotten along but one thing they had agreed on was the correct way to praise the Lord.

The problem was the house. If she left Marty and his friends alone God knows what she would find when she came home. She poured a cup of coffee and sat down to read the *Sisters' Gazette*. In the back she noticed an ad in the 'Work Wanted' section for a house cleaner. She wouldn't even have to be up to her standards; just good enough to keep the house from becoming a disaster. She dialed the number before she could talk herself out of it. Brianna could start on Monday.

Good, she could make sure the girl was decent enough and then pack and leave. She would deal with the scofflaws across the street when she came home. She hadn't forgotten that snippy little bitch, excuse her language dear Lord, but the bitch would have to wait. Mrs. Fowler was going to take a vacation.

Out in the barn Jason had deposited the box of supplies on an old chest freezer and surveyed the progress Marty and Gordon had made. They still had a long way to go and the barn was freezing even with four space heaters and he couldn't stand the volume on the boom box. He crossed over to it to turn the volume down and stepped on the wood panel over the old well. It gave more than a little and his heart skipped a beat.

"You know we really need to put a better cover over this well. I don't tread water that great."

"Pussy. Why don't you make that your job? Right now I need to figure out how to get the Freon out of these refrigerators."

"I thought you said it was easy."

"Fuck you. Why don't you do something for a change instead of parking your ass there with your thumb up your nose." The hostility in Gordon's voice got Jason to wondering the wisdom of the whole enterprise. He was still working his job at the waste management plant in Bend and even if it was stinky at times it paid well enough. Maybe he shouldn't have let Marty get him mixed up with Gordon. Gordon came with a lot of baggage—none of it good.

Jason started rummaging around in the toolbox and found a tape measure. He measured the wood panel over the wellhead and started repeating to himself "six by five, six by five" since he didn't have anything to write it down on. He would drive into Bend and get a heavy sheet of plywood. He could get it covered Monday after work. He had to help his Dad lay a new vinyl floor in his trailer this weekend. And his mother was complaining about a toilet. He loved his parents but they sure liked to get their pound of flesh. It was the only thing that made the barn enterprise tempting; a chance to get away. Maybe Phoenix or something. He heard a lot of good things about Arizona on the radio. Like that sheriff. Of course he wouldn't do any shit like this down there. He heard the guy made the jailbirds wear pink underwear and eat baloney for breakfast, lunch, and dinner. That guy had a pair and made all the weinie liberals cry in their craft beer.

Chapter Nine

The girl on the porch had long straggly orange hair and a vicious-looking cold sore on her mouth. Mrs. Fowler almost sent her away but she was desperate so she opened the door and Brianna slouched in. She hadn't brought any of her own cleaning supplies; she said that most of her clients preferred her to use their own. That didn't sound unreasonable to Mrs. Fowler so she showed her where the vacuum was and gave her a list of what she wanted done. Then she planted herself in front of the TV and started watching reruns of that poor Paula Deen. During the commercial breaks she checked on the girl's progress. She was not a speed demon but she seemed to do an adequate job. Not as good as Mrs. Fowler would like in a permanent cleaner but she would do in the interim.

The girl was cleaning in the kitchen when Marty came in from the barn and started making sandwiches. Mrs. Fowler noticed he took a very long time making four sandwiches. There was a lot of giggling coming from the kitchen and Mrs. Fowler decided it was time to make fresh coffee. That put the kibosh on giggling and wrapped up the sandwich-making pronto. She wasn't paying the girl to flirt with her son. And she had to point out some dirt on the kitchen cabinets that the girl had missed. Maybe this wasn't a good idea. But she had her bags packed in her bedroom and Pooh was all excited about going for a trip. He always liked trips in the car although there wouldn't be any open windows to drool out of on this trip. It was too cold for that, and did she pack both his little coats? She went to check. Brianna thanked God the old witch was not going to be around the next week when she came.

At the end of four hours Mrs. Fowler paid her off and arranged the next time so she would be sure that Marty was home to let her in. The girl drove off in an old orange Datsun and Mrs. Fowler did a complete inspection of her work. She made notes on the list of tasks where she thought Brianna could make improvements. There were lots of notes. Maybe she should go over the list with Marty. It was after four now; maybe they could take a break.

She loaded up a plate of cookies and pulled her coat and

boots on. Pooh slipped out of the door with her. He was going to freeze without his coat, the naughty boy. Well it would be a little warmer in the barn. It was quiet; the torturous music wasn't grinding out of cracks in the barn door. She stood inside, allowing her eyes to adjust to the dim light. No one was there. They must have gone out without her noticing. There was a funny smell in the air. Pooh was barking at something in the rear of the barn—probably just one of the old freezers but she went towards his bouncing little form.

She stubbed her foot on an old wood panel and sprawled out on what she remembered was the cover over the old wellhead—the one her ex-husband had never repaired, the bastard, excuse me Jesus. There was an ominous crack and the wood seemed to give a little, then it gave a lot, and then Mrs. Fowler and ragged bits of the old cover went crashing down fifty feet to the bottom of the well. The water level wasn't deep, only four feet or so, but unfortunately Mrs. Fowler had been knocked out on the way down and ended up semi-submerged upside down in the cold water. She didn't really feel a thing as she effortlessly drowned.

Above, Pooh was circling the hole and barking in heightened hysteria, but then he discovered the spilled cookies and gave it a rest. He would wait for Mommy to come back up and let him back in the house. After a while he heard Marty's pick-up pull in and he raced out and made it just in time for Marty to let him in the front door.

Marty called for his mother but she didn't answer. The

door to her bedroom was closed so he supposed she was laying down for a nap. He went into the kitchen and opened
the refrigerator. His mother had stocked up on his favorite
things, which was really very nice of her. He took a cold roast
chicken out and stood at the counter pulling off chunks of
meat. That girl had done a nice job in the kitchen. She was
kind of cute and she laughed at his jokes, which didn't happen
all that often. Maybe next week when his mom wasn't around
he could talk to her more. He heard Jason's pick-up pull up
and he watched Jason pull a plywood board out of the back of
his pick-up. Good, let him do the heavy lifting for a change.
He opened a can of beer and went into the livingroom and
turned on the TV.

Jason struggled to get the heavy piece of plywood into the
barn and set it down by the open well.

"Jeez, that's deep." Jason peered into the black hole. It was
kind of creepy. He picked up a couple of loose pieces of
wood and dropped them down the hole. Then he noticed
an upended ceramic plate off to the side and he picked it
up. Underneath was an oatmeal raisin cookie that Pooh had
missed. Jason stared at the cookie. He stared at the open pit.
Something didn't seem right. He felt a sudden chill up his
back and he turned and ran from the barn. He let himself
into the kitchen; he could hear the TV in the livingroom.

"Marty, where's your mom?" Jason tried to sound noncha-
lant.

"Taking a nap, I think." Marty was flipping through the

stations. Jason walked down the hall and went into the bathroom. After standing there a moment he flushed the toilet and
opened the door. He glanced back to the livingroom and then
poked his head in the doorway of Mrs. Fowler's bedroom.
The bed was empty and neatly made. He went back to the
kitchen and stared at the half empty package of cookies on
the counter. He was getting a very bad feeling about this. He
opened the door to the garage and could see Mrs. Fowler's
car sitting in the darkness.

He went back out to the barn with Pooh at his heels. The
little dog went right up to the hole and looked down expectantly. Jason peered down into the depths but couldn't see a
thing. He found a flashlight and pointed it down. He could
just make out the cracked boards. He flashed the light around
the floor of the barn looking for clues and there to the left
of the well was a woman's shoe. A sensible black, size nine.
Jason was paralyzed. He didn't know what to do. He went
back into the kitchen and used the landline to call Gordon.

"Hello, Mrs. Fowler, how are you today?" Gordon's greeting
was based on the caller ID and his usual smarmy assumption
that old people couldn't see what a lying piece of shit he was.

Jason hesitated and then seemed to gargle into the phone,
"Ah dude, we've got a situation here."

"What now?"

"We've got a big problem, dude."

"Shit, I'm not Houston, you know. Can't you guys figure

anything out for yourselves? I've got other irons in the fire right now."

"Marty's mom fell down the well." Jason whispered.

"What? I can't hear you."

"Marty's mom fell down the well." Jason pitched his voice slightly higher and glanced nervously towards the livingroom.

"What the fuck? Is she okay?"

"Fuck no, Gordon, she's not okay. What do you think? She's an old lady and she fell maybe a hundred feet into a well." Jason was suddenly very angry.

"What do the ambulance guys say?"

"Shit, man, I didn't call any ambulance, she's still in the well. She's dead. She's drowned. She's like that guy on the Titanic. She's …"

"Okay, I get it man." Gordon paused to think. "How's Marty taking it?"

"Well at last the great Gordo thinks of someone other than himself. Marty doesn't know. He's watching TV and drinking. Jesus, he's going to kill us when he finds out."

"How the fuck do you figure it's our fault? You were the one who was supposed to fix the cover on the well. Shit, I told you to fix it! Don't go blaming me if you fuckups didn't like put safety first. Damn, that could have been me in the well. Any one of us could have …"

"Shut the fuck up, Gordon. We need to figure out what to do now." Jason's fear erupted in rage and for once he had Gordon a little cowed.

"I was just saying."

"Well, try thinking for once before you go blowing off your mouth. We need to try to stay cool." Jason peeked into the living room to see if Marty was listening but he was heavily involved in a *Price is Right* negotiation.

"We don't need the police climbing all over that barn. Not until we get a couple of batches done and we have enough money to relocate."

"You mean just leave her down there? And you say I'm cold. Jesus, Jason, I don't think Marty will go for that."

"I just got an idea. We don't tell him. He's half loaded now. I can slip him an Oxy and when he wakes up in the morning we can tell him she left on that trip she was talking about. He'll probably be relieved that he doesn't have to worry about her finding out what we're doing in the barn."

"You're crazy. No wait. Fuck, that's not a bad idea." Gordon thought for a moment. "Good. Go out and cover that stupid well. I'm on my way. I need to think this through. Go give him that Oxy and a shot of vodka or something. We need to keep him out of it till we clean this up." Gordon hung up.

Jason went out to his car and pulled the Oxy out from under the passenger seat. He had a nearly full bottle of vodka in the trunk and he took it in to Marty who was delighted by this turn of events. Jason left him with the bottle of vodka and went back into the barn. The barn weirded him out; he stood in the now darkened doorway and stared towards the back. What if she was just knocked out? He didn't want to nail the new cover in place—not by himself. He went back to the house and searched for a better flashlight. He was retrieving a hammer and some nails from his truck when Gordon pulled up.

"Where's Marty?" Gordon asked as he followed Jason back to the barn.

"He's asleep on the couch. I don't think he's coming out of it till morning." Jason stood at the edge of the well and the two men peered down as he aimed the flashlight into the dark hole.

"I don't see nothing. Are you sure the old crone is down there?"

"Don't call her that. Show some respect." Jason wanted to crack the flashlight upside Gordon's head.

"Shit, is that a foot there, over to the left by that broken board? Man, what a fucking way to go. Trip on a board and then splash, head first in a well."

Solemnly the two men looked at the confirmation that Mrs. Fowler had indeed met her untimely end at the bottom of the well.

"I don't think this is the trip she had in mind." Gordon giggled and Jason slapped him with the flashlight.

"Help me nail this down. Good thing it's winter. It's too cold for her to smell much." Jason was grasping the new piece of plywood and Gordon gave a hand. When it was firmly nailed down Jason stood silently. He wasn't sure if maybe they should say a prayer but he didn't know any.

Back in the house they checked to see if Marty was awake. He wasn't. In the kitchen Jason laid out the plan. They would load up Mrs. Fowler's suitcase in the car and Gordon would drive it out to one of the forest service roads in the Deschutes National Forest. Jason would follow and they would leave it in a ditch or something. When Marty woke up they would act like nothing had happened and Jason would tell him that his mother had left a little early. Then they would get a couple of batches cooked up. By the time the car was found in the spring it would just look like she got lost and made the mistake of leaving her car. People did that all the time; the forest was probably littered with bodies that were never found.

And it wasn't as if one of them had shoved her into the well. It was just a tragic accident. Time to move on.

The next morning Marty woke with a blinding headache and didn't feel able to crawl out of bed and climb the stairs until mid-afternoon. Thirst and a bursting bladder forced him finally to brave the upstairs and the assuredly nasty disapproval of his mother. After a long visit to the bathroom he went into the kitchen for some orange juice. No sound from his mother so she must be out. He drank directly from the carton and contemplated life. With his mother gone it would be easier for them to produce the meth in the barn. And he planned on getting better acquainted with that housecleaner. Boy, was he fucked up. He couldn't even remember why he had drunk so much. Jason had given him something too.

With the random drug tests as a condition of his probation he had stayed relatively free of shit. His tolerance must have gone way down.

He went into the livingroom and stood in his jockeys staring out the window. He turned to go back downstairs and stepped into a large wet spot on the carpet. Fucking little dog. He shouted for the dog but the little shit was hiding somewhere. If the little turd was going to start pissing in the house his mother was going to have to do something. Disgusting little shit.

He was coming upstairs when he heard the backdoor open but it was Gordon and Jason and not his mom. They stood talking in the kitchen while Marty rummaged in the refrigerator. He made a liverwurst sandwich and drank half a carton of milk. Jason had gone to the bathroom while he stood over the sink eating. Gordon was talking about distribution networks and he wasn't really tracking it. Gordon took the hint and stopped.

Jason came out of the bathroom and gave a guilty look down the hall to Mrs. Fowler's room. In the livingroom the empty vodka bottle had rolled under the coffee table and he bent to pick it up. That's when he found Mrs. Fowler's purse tucked up under an end table. He picked it up but he could hear Marty in the kitchen telling Gordon he would meet them in the barn after he took a piss. Jason looked around wildly and pushed the purse in the only hiding place—behind the couch. It would be safe there for now.

As agreed, it was Gordon out in the barn who mentioned that they had come by for him in the morning and his mom had said he was ill. She said she couldn't wait any longer; she needed to get on her way to visit her sister. She would call later to see how he was. Marty seemed okay with that and they set to work setting up their new enterprise.

Claudie stood for a moment to get her bearings. It was her favorite kind of bookstore. A little cramped with wooden floors and not a lot of fluff, like racks of funny greeting cards and cutesy stuffed animals. A tall man with brown hair was doodling at the counter and barely looked up when she came in. She steered to the Travel section as usual on the outside chance that her little book was in stock. It had been out of print for twenty years, but you never know. It wasn't there of course. Ah, vanity.

She went to the Thriller section of the used paperbacks next, looking for something different. She wasn't in the mood for anything literary, just a fast page-turner, but she didn't see anything that interested her. She rounded a bookcase and spied the historical fiction aisle. Most of them were bodice rippers but at the bottom it looked like there were one or two Dorothy Dunnett paperbacks. She reached down and tugged one out but as she straightened up she felt a very familiar and disconcerting shift in her lower back.

"Oh damn," she groaned and stood absolutely still for a few minutes.

"Are you okay?" She looked over at the man who now stood at the end of the aisle clutching a sheaf of papers. He looked slightly annoyed by the interruption.

"It's ah," she gasped a little, "my back is … do you have a chair I could sit in?"

"Yes, of course. In the back." He paused and then said, "Do you, ah, want me to bring it to you?"

"No, no I can walk. I just need a moment to rest." She took baby steps and followed him towards the rear of the store. "I hate to be a bother." She gratefully sank into a leather chair. Her back hurt like a son-of-a-bitch but she tried to smile, a rather ghastly attempt that seemed to alarm the man more. She felt like an utter fool, an old fool.

The man was watching her from the front counter; he apparently decided that more was in order. He walked back and asked, "I was going to make a cup of tea, would you like some?"

Claudie nodded and the man disappeared into another room. She could hear him fill a kettle and pull some cups out of a cabinet. The little sitting area in the rear of the store had shelves of older rare books.

"Maybe you'd like an aspirin and some water?"

"Excellent, couldn't hurt. Is this your store?"

"No, just watching it for a friend who's recovering from surgery." He came out with the water and aspirin.

She swallowed and handed the glass back. "Thank you. My name is Claudie."

"Frank. I'll be right back with the tea, Claudie."

Claudie was still holding the Dorothy Dunnett novel but one of the older books on the shelf beside her caught her eye. Wilkie Collins' *Woman in White*. She reached for it with only a minor twinge in her back. It was a first edition and a little spendy. It had been a long time since she had read his books. She opened to the first page and was reading when Frank returned with the tea. He set it down on the table beside her along with some milk and sugar. He glanced down on the book and Claudie caught a flicker, his eyebrows rose up and down quickly with a hint of distain.

"Not a fan of Collins?"

"No. I find most nineteenth-century English novels a bit overblown."

"So not a fan of Dickens?"

"God no. A glorified dime novelist."

"Austen?"

"She's an exception. More late-eighteenth century to my mind. I much prefer Swift, Lawrence Sterne, and Defoe. Now Defoe could write an adventure novel. Much superior to Collins claptrap. I teach Intro to the Early English Novel."

"Ah, an academic. Do you teach at the community college in Bend?"

Frank's lip curled and those eyebrows did another dance. "Lord no. I'm on the faculty of the University of Wisconsin."

He hesitated, "Currently I'm on a sabbatical. I'm helping my sister; she's recovering from a medical emergency."

"How good of you."

The bell on the front door tinkled and Claudie could see a woman drift down a couple of aisles. Frank went back to the front counter but paid no attention to the woman and she left without buying anything. Claudie was grateful for the tea but on the whole Frank's attention to the business of running the store seemed a little lax. And his superior attitude towards other people's reading tastes was not going to be conducive to brisk sales. The owner of the store was in danger of finding that his Christmas season was very lean this year.

Claudie finished her tea and could feel that the aspirin and brief rest had relaxed her back sufficiently that she felt she could trust it enough to make it to her car and go home. She thanked Frank for his hospitality but he paid little notice; he was busy drawing something with colored pencils at the front counter.

When she got home and slowly eased out of the car she hoped that Mrs. Fowler was watching. Today she really did look like a feeble old woman.

The only one who watched her painful exit from the car was Mrs. Boyle who had dropped by to ostensibly check on Mrs. O'Brien's wellbeing. She pulled in behind Claudie and got out in time to offer to help carry in her groceries. Claudie was in too much pain to object but once inside her apartment she regretted her moment of weakness.

"My aunt had a bad back too. It gave her endless pain and boy did we hear about it. You couldn't shut her up. You just sit down and relax. You should think about going to an acupuncturist. I have some herbal tea in my car that can work miracles too. I could get some for you to try." Mrs. Boyle took the opportunity to open a few cupboards. Snooping, Claudie thought.

"Don't bother yourself. I really don't need anything. Was there a reason for you dropping by?" What Claudie wanted was for Mrs. Boyle to be gone so she could pour a glass of wine.

Mrs. Boyle was now emptying the grocery bag and scrutinizing each item.

"You know you can buy jam that's as good as this at Trader Joe's in Bend. Cost you a whole lot less." She examined the price tag on a package of cheese and shook her head.

"Mrs. Boyle, please don't trouble yourself. I'm sure you're a busy woman and I don't want to keep you."

Mrs. Boyle raised her gaze and looked at Claudie speculatively. She certainly didn't look very formidable right now. She noticed a flash at the window, a bit of sunlight suddenly reflected off the window of a truck pulling into the house across the street. A man with his hair pulled back in a ponytail and wearing a scrungy brown jacket got out of the truck and went into the house. She looked back at Claudie and realized it was ridiculous to have even given an atom of credence to Corrine Bales. It was really very silly of her.

"Mrs. O'Brien, I was concerned because I haven't heard back from you. I've written and called several times and when you didn't respond I became worried. The hospital feels very strongly that …"

Claudie broke in, "The hospital wants to make sure I'm not going to follow through on my threat to sue. Don't worry, Mrs. Boyle, I have no intention of pursuing the matter further. Now if you don't mind I really would like to lie down."

"Thank you, Mrs. O'Brien. I'll tell the Director that there is nothing to be concerned about." She walked to the door and then glanced around the cozy room. "This is really a nice little apartment you have here. It was very nice of your niece to give you such a snug little place."

"My niece? Oh yes, she did a remarkable job converting the garage. I'm very comfortable." Claudie waited for Mrs. Boyle to get the hell out of her apartment but Mrs. Boyle had paused at the door with a frown on her face.

"Goodbye."

"Uh, yes, goodbye."

Mrs. Boyle shut the door behind her and walked to her car. The house across the street looked like an old farmhouse. It sat a little way back from the road on a few acres. She could just glimpse an old barn set back behind it. Mrs. Boyle started her car and pulled out slowly; as she backed into the street she could see the mailbox at the end of the driveway. Fowler. Oh Christ. This was crazy. Converted garages were not unusual; old ladies did not plot foul murders because of them, and

Fowler, Fowl, foul. Well it was just stupid. She wasn't going to spend any more time on this foolishness. She sped down the street. It was Friday and she was off for the weekend. She looked forward to getting to her little oasis of spiritual calm. In an hour she would be transformed back into her true incarnation, Sonia, seer into the mysterious realms of other planes of existence.

"Maddie, what's with the word of the week? Prevaricator? Do all the words have to have some dark bent to them?" Peter looked at his daughter who was preoccupied with her tablet. "If I ask you a question I expect a response young lady."

"It's just a suggestion from Mrs. Williams, my English teacher. We're studying the treatment of strong female characters in eighteenth-century literature. Do you know that if a woman became 'inconvenient' for her husband he could have her committed to an insane asylum? Too bad you can't do that for Chrystal."

"Knock it off, Maddie." He immediately felt bad. It had come out too harsh. It was so hard now. Every parent he knew who had teenagers talked about the metamorphosis that seemed to turn their sweet children into prickly ferrets.

"You used to really like Chrystal. What happened? You know she's really trying hard but you don't seem to see it."

"What *you* don't see is how she treats you. She's wrapped

you around her little finger. Look around at all the changes she's made. Next thing you know she's going to want to upgrade us for newer and flashier model children. I can't conform to what Chrystal thinks is the perfect young teen-ager." Maddie slid off the kitchen stool and started to leave the kitchen. The conversation was not one she was interested in continuing.

"Wait." Maddie paused at the door but didn't turn.

"Chrystal has been having trouble with her laptop. You wouldn't know anything about that would you?"

"Dad, I don't touch her stuff. Maybe she picked up some virus from one of those weird exercise videos that she streams. She was doing something called Tantric Yoga the other day. Why does she always have to be so weird? Why can't she do American Yoga, for God's sake?" Maddie escaped up the stairs.

American Yoga. Huh. Peter opened Chrystal's laptop and turned it on and then typed in her password. The screen opened and he could see the first problem. He doubted that Chrystal would have a picture of zombies feasting on hapless old people as the screen background. He powered it down. He didn't have a clue about computer viruses.

The woman who looked up when Claudie entered Liz's Cut-n-Go had what appeared to be a giant hairball sprouting off the side of her head. With ribbons. She was encased in a flowing crimson and gold robe and if this was the hairdresser that Chrystal had recommended, then she thought Chrystal was having a little fun with her.

The woman turned and said something to another woman sitting behind her and then sailed past Claudie. In a strange way she looked familiar but Claudie couldn't imagine why. The remaining woman, somewhere in her hefty forties but carrying it well, stood and welcomed Claudie. Claudie sat in the proffered chair with relief and told her she just needed a haircut.

"You new in town or just visiting?" Liz was running her hands through Claudie's hair and studying it and her face.

"New. You might say an extended visit. I haven't decided." She was led back to a wash station and had her head vigorously scrubbed before returning to the chair.

"I was curious—who was the woman who just left? The one in the red dress?"

"Oh that's just Sonia. She has the shop next door." Liz paused and looked at Claudie through the mirror, "I don't do Sonia's hair. That's a creation all her own." They both smiled. "Sonia's one of the local characters, real nice mind you. She adds a lot of color to the town. She does psychic readings on the weekends. I've known her since junior high and she's always been into that spooky stuff. She was a Goth in high school, dyed her hair black with a maroon streak. Then she went to college and got into all this ooga booga stuff like crystals and reincarnation. She works in Bend during the week at a real job and then on the weekends the business suit comes off—watch out."

Claudie laughed, "I had a husband who was into that all that stuff. He said he could turn himself into a coyote, a Native American symbol of transformation he said. I think his transformation had a lot more to do with the magic mushrooms he'd eat than anything else that I could see. I looked it up after he transformed into a missing husband and it was more likely he was the trickster of Indian legend than anything else."

"He ran off?"

"Yep. Poof—he was gone."

"Maybe Sonia could find him for you." Liz laughed.

"God no. It's been thirty years. I'd pay her to lose him again."

Liz laughed, "She'd probably make more money helping some of the women who come in here lose their husbands than keep them. The things you hear in this chair you wouldn't believe. I'm just glad my husband still has his job and doesn't complain about taking out the garbage."

"Sounds like a jewel."

"Yeah." Liz clipped steady for several minutes then asked, "You living in town or renting one of the vacation homes towards Black Butte?"

"I'm in town. I'm renting from Chrystal Walker. She's the one who recommended you to me." Claudie winced. She probably shouldn't have said that. She was supposed to be a relative, not a renter.

"Ah Chrystal. She married the vice-principal of the high school after his first wife died. I didn't know they had apartments to rent."

"Actually I'm not renting. I'm related to Peter's father's aunt and they're letting me live in the garage they remodeled into an apartment. I have a medical condition and they're helping me." She prayed the lie would cover her faux pas.

"That's sweet of Peter. He was always a generous guy. Oh jeez, did you say garage? That's funny. There was a lady in here last week who was going on about some converted garage where someone was going to be murdered. Boy was she wound up. TJ, he's a friend of Peter's, brought her in. Corrine is his aunt, poor man. She was in a coma and apparently dreamed some strange things while she was down. I guess they can do that. Well, she's having a hard time coming to grips with reality. Although there are plenty of people in town who never felt she had much of a grip before. Anyway, she's convinced that two women were in her hospital room plotting to kill another woman in a converted garage. It was crazy! I couldn't shut her up. I have a hard time keeping a straight face sometimes. People really will believe anything I guess."

Conversation was halted as Liz set to work drying and styling Claudie's hair. Claudie tried to make sense of what Liz had to say about Corrine Bales. The name seemed familiar but she couldn't quite put a finger on it. Well, every town had a few nuts in it. On her way out Liz called out, "You be careful in that garage." They both laughed.

Back home she had barely taken off her coat when there was a frantic pounding on her door. She opened it to find Maddie almost in tears.

"Claudie, please, you have to help me. I think I broke the washing machine. There are suds coming out everywhere."

Claudie followed her into the kitchen to the corner where the washer and dryer were normally hidden behind louvered doors. Sam was standing in a mountain of bubbles and laughing as he swatted puffballs of them around the room. He was not taking the disaster as seriously as his sister. The washer was silent but red lights were lit up all over the control panel.

"What happened?"

"I needed to do some clothes and we were out of laundry soap. So I used the dishwasher soap."

"Oops. Not good. How much did you use? Never mind. Any is too much."

The bubbles were sliding across the floor in big waves of white and in a bit they would be soaking into the livingroom carpet.

"Sam, get the broom and let's try sweeping them out the back door. Maddie, go get some towels—big ones."

Between the three of them they got the sudsy mess out the door and Claudie contemplated the clothes still in the washer. Fortunately it was a light load and they used a laundry basket to transfer them to the kitchen sink. Maddie began the process of rinsing them out and Claudie ran the washer on the rinse cycle to try to clean the suds out. It took three cycles to get the suds down to a level the washer would tolerate.

The kitchen floor was spotless when they finished. After Claudie left, Maddie and Sam made a pact not to speak of this. They also decided to stop calling Claudie "coly" behind her back. She really wasn't that much of a crazy old lady.

Maddie's new word for the week was drudge.

Chapter Ten

"Here, Sam. Take this out to the trash and bury it deep." Claudie handed Sam a brown bag and returned to chopping onions.

"What's in it?" Sam asked as he opened the door to a cold blast of wind.

"Evidence." Claudie laughed. "It's the packaging from the sausages and other verboten ingredients. I don't want Chrystal finding them."

"Won't she notice when she tastes stuff?" Sam looked very doubtful that Claudie's scheme to serve edible appetizers at the party would go unnoticed.

"She's dieting again. She's going to stick to the crudités.

You're letting in winter—close the door."

Claudie dumped the onions in the fry pan with a goodly dollop of olive oil. She wiped her eyes and then checked the recipe. Sausage-stuffed mushrooms were in her repertoire of quick and easy hors d'oeuvres, always a hit at her long ago Christmas parties.

Sam returned and stood watching her. "What are crudités?"

"Raw vegies. Okay, kitchen helper, no standing around idle. Take those carrots, broccoli, and tomatoes, and arrange them on that platter." In answer to his quizzical look she added, "Like in rows of soldiers standing in army platoons. And then take this parsley and stick it around the edges."

"Why?"

"That's what you do at fancy parties. Everything's dressed up including the vegetables. When you're done with that do the same thing with the fruit I cut up."

The door to the living room opened and Maddie came in wearing a bright green party dress with a surplus of ruffles. Claudie hesitated before saying anything. She knew the dress would be a sore topic but Sam had no similar inhibition, and when he looked up he gave one high whoop before Maddie slugged him, resoundingly on his arm.

"Children! Stop or I'll send you back to the adults. Maddie, how many guests have arrived?"

"I don't know, about a dozen. TJ, his father, and Chrystal's mother—she brought a date."

"Eew!" Sam paused in his vegetable arranging to contemplate such an old person on a date.

"I know, gross, and a tall snooty lady, MJ something. I think she's Chrystal's boss at the real estate company." Maddie watched as Claudie mixed the sausage and onions with other ingredients and began stuffing the mushrooms.

"Maddie, be a dear and take that tray of vegies out and check to see if the cheese and crackers need replenishing." Claudie opened the oven, tucked the mushrooms in, and then started working on the salmon platter. She spooned a smidgeon of an orange miso sauce on each bite and then sprinkled sesame seeds over the top. Sam watched as she tucked more parsley around the edges.

"Did you make anything a kid might like?"

"You mean like you? Something like deviled eggs?"

Sam brightened and Claudie pulled a tray out of the refrigerator.

"What's this red stuff on them?"

"That's just paprika. Take this tray out. I have another batch without the red stuff for you two."

Alone for a few minutes, Claudie took the bottle of Champagne that she had reserved for herself out of the fridge and topped off her glass. Things were on schedule, she hadn't cut or burned herself, at least not yet, and she hadn't had to spend time talking to people she wasn't interested in. This could end up being one of her best Christmas parties.

She was glad that she had volunteered to help Peter with the party. The kids had reported the ongoing argument between Chrystal and their father. Peter liked to do two parties a year: a summer barbeque and a Christmas party.

Chrystal flat out told him that she was too busy with two jobs to go to all that work. Not that she was working that much in the current real estate market, but she was spending a lot of time at Six Firs. Her disinterest lasted until she found out that Claudie was doing the cooking. Then she was all over the menu and the importance of serving healthy vegetarian food. People just ruined themselves over the holidays, gorging on all the sugar and fattening treats, don't you know? She found the time to shop for soy cheese, tofu, and an array of fruits and vegetables. She would find the soy products in the refrigerator the day after the party.

In the living room Maddie was being interrogated by a succession of adults all inquiring about her school, the usual dreary stuff, what grade was she in, and what did she like. It was all so boring. She retreated to the corner by the tree but she was not allowed to be in peace. TJ's father at least did not recite the litany of grown-up questions; he was treating her like an adult, almost a co-conspirator with his sly digs at the other adults, especially Chrystal. She was giggling so hard that she had tears in her eyes when TJ joined them.

"Hey Dad, a minute?" TJ gripped his father's upper arm and pulled him towards the hallway.

"What that fuck was that?"

"What?" Frank looked surprised.

"Maddie is fourteen. Fourteen. You do not lean in to my

friend's fourteen-year-old daughter unless you want to go to jail."

"I wasn't leaning into her, I was just talking. Jeez." Frank shook off his son's hand and returned to the other guests. TJ was entirely too full of himself. Just because he was a little down on his luck that didn't mean his son could presume to dictate his behavior. He must have been talking to his mother. That vengeful bitch. Frank poured himself another scotch and tried to shake off the negative vibrations. He was just going to have to admit that he had reared a moron. The bitch had fostered his son's ego with the expectation he deserved a blue ribbon just for showing up. Life didn't work that way. You could labor your whole life building a body of work and achievements, and then one little bimbo misses her period and sends it all tumbling down the crapper.

He looked at the other females at the party. The only decent looking one was the hostess and she was probably off limits too. There was her mother who wasn't bad looking for her age, sixty maybe, but you would need a trowel to scrape the makeup off and god only knew what you would find under-neath. Besides, she had a date who appeared to be following the hostess with his eyes and paying scant attention to the mother. Interesting. Chrystal was studiously avoiding the guy, Ray? Definitely something going on there. That left the tall elegant looking woman who kept checking her watch as if timing how long she needed to stay. It looked like she was un-easy socializing with the hoi polloi. MJ something, Chrystal's real estate boss. Maybe he could get that tight-assed smile off her face. Sometimes broads like that were really hot in bed.

Maddie returned to the living room with the platter of salmon that was immediately swarmed over. The next delicacy was the stuffed mushrooms. Chrystal was telling everybody how most of the food was vegan and it just went to prove that you could eat healthy and responsibly over the holidays and still eat delicious food.

TJ had gulped down two of the mushrooms before Chrystal made her pronouncement and he looked down at the little crumble of sausage on his plate. Definitely meat sausage. He looked over to Peter who was suppressing a smirk. Peter cocked his head towards the kitchen and TJ followed him in where he found the two kids and Claudie huddled over another tray of food.

"Weinie bites. You've been hiding the good stuff." He helped himself to one of the small delicacies. "Once again you've saved the day, Claudie. I regret now that I ate before I came. No offense, Peter—Chrystal isn't known for her kitchen prowess.

"I hope you still have a little room. You two can help by taking out the ham and scalloped potatoes."

"Good lord. Even Chrystal's going to notice that ham isn't on the vegan list."

"I'll pour her another Chardonnay and she'll be fine. Are you kids doing okay?"

Maddie nodded and Sam gave his dad a thumb's up. After

the men carried the new trays of food out, the kids polished off the mini-hot dogs baked in buttery soft bread.

"Now who's interested in cookies?" Claudie asked.

An hour later the kids had gone to bed but the party was still limping towards the finish line. Claudie had washed up as best she could and was getting ready to slip back over to her apartment. Outside she paused to look at the clear star-studded sky. Orion was still visible and there was no moon to dim the starlight. She heard her name called and she looked back in the kitchen window. It was Chrystal, and Claudie stepped back away from the light coming out of the window. It had been a good night and she didn't want Chrystal to destroy the mild glow she had going.

Inside Chrystal stood by the refrigerator seemingly lost in thought. The door between the kitchen and the living room opened again and an older man stepped in and quickly closed the door behind him. Without hesitation he encircled Chrystal's waist with an arm and swung her in for a deep kiss. Claudie watched with interest. She hadn't been kissed like that for years. Dispassionately she tried to determine if she missed all that. Mid-thought she came back to the present circumstances—that Chrystal was energetically kissing someone who was not Peter. The stupid slut had invited her lover to the family Christmas party.

She waited for them to come up for air or for someone to walk in on them. That would be entertaining but not very enjoyable for Peter. It would definitely dim the Christmas spirit. The two finally separated and Claudie could get a clear look at the man. He had to be sixty if he was a day. Good looking, he reminded her a little of someone. Just then Elaine opened the door and the two stepped apart before she caught sight of them. Now this was interesting. Didn't Maddie say Elaine came with a date? Layers of interesting. Elaine claimed the man's hand and went back into the party room.

Chrystal turned toward the kitchen window and leaned towards it to see her reflection. She wiped a finger along her lower lip to clear up the mussed up lipstick and then her eyes swiveled in Claudie's direction. Claudie froze. She couldn't tell if Chrystal had seen her; there had been no reaction. Chrystal returned to the party and Claudie opened her apartment door.

Back inside the house she remembered her bottle of Champagne. Not much left but she wanted it to finish this intriguing evening. In the kitchen she had just pulled the bottle out when the kitchen door opened again and she was face to face with the older man. He gave her a brief glance and then seeing that Chrystal was not in the room he retreated through the door. Claudie was left holding the bottle of Champagne and remembering where she had seen this man before. It was going to take more than this little bit of wine to digest this new turn. The last time she saw Ray was in London when he said he was going out for a walk. Thirty years is a long walk.

For most of Claudie's adult life Christmas had been relatively free of stress; a lack of children and nearby relatives had allowed her to make it a special time focused on holiday decorating, cooking, and dinners with friends. It was only in the last few years as friends died or moved on that the season had become something she observed like through a store plate glass window: all the warmth and merriment on the other side of the glass. This year, if she was looking through a glass at the Walker family, she was happy that all the Sturm und Drang was on the other side.

At the Christmas party she hadn't paid much attention to Elaine, Chrystal's mother. She had noticed the sparkly dress and jewelry and the oddness of her face. At first she assumed it was the dramatic application of her makeup. Now she had concluded that Elaine had made an unfortunate choice of plastic surgeons. The doctor had puffed her cheeks up so much that to say she was apple-cheeked would not have been an exaggeration. Large apples. And she was always smiling. It took a while to adjust to the ear-to-ear grin that never went away. It almost looked painful. Although Elaine had a house in Sun River, she spent a few days after the Christmas party at the Walker house. What little time Claudie was exposed to her made Claudie a little more sympathetic to Chrystal.

She wasn't too sure what was going on with Maddie, except that she had become completely intolerable around Chrystal.

This created all sorts of anxiety for Sam, and Peter was wearing out from refereeing the squabbles. Chrystal's mother Elaine had no inhibitions about stirring up the pot.

One day Maddie knocked on her door and asked if she could hang around. She needed to escape what she called the 'evil twins.' She promised to be quiet as a mouse and for a while she sat at the little table in Claudie's kitchenette area and worked on her laptop. But it was impossible for her to hold in her teenage angst.

"They're like stupid high school girls. Every time I go into the kitchen they're sitting there and they stop talking when I come in. It's like they're talking about me all the time."

"Maybe it's not about you. Maybe they're just talking grown-up stuff that they don't want you to hear."

"Yeah, but I bet Chrystal isn't telling her mom that she's fooling around with that guru guy." Maddie's hand clamped onto her mouth and she looked stricken and guilty at the same time.

"How do you know this, Maddie? This isn't anything you should be poking your nose into."

"Why not? She's making a fool of Dad. He hasn't a clue. It's disgusting what she says to that creep. He's so old. How can she stand it?" Maddie stopped because it finally dawned on her that she had said too much.

"Maddie? How is it exactly that you know this? Claudie sat down at the table with her. Maddie made an involuntary motion to close her laptop.

"You're not getting into her emails are you?"

Maddie's eyes widened a little and she gave a small shake of her head.

"Because if you are you could get into a lot of trouble." Claudie paused searching for a way to reach the girl. "There are times when you don't want to get in the middle of other people's problems. Have you ever heard the phrase, 'don't shoot the messenger?' Grown-ups have to work this stuff out by themselves. You don't—trust me on this—want to get in the middle of it."

"How can Dad work it out if he doesn't even know it's going on?"

"I have an old theory about this. Give a man, or in this case a woman, enough rope and they'll hang themselves." Maddie looked doubtful about this wisdom. "What I'm saying is that if Chrystal is doing something she shouldn't it will come out eventually. You just have to be patient."

Maddie rolled her eyes and then opened the laptop up again and turned it towards Claudie. "What about this old guy Ray? I've been looking him up on the Internet and something isn't right, I know it. I can't find anything about him and his big spiritual movement that's older than 2010. It's like he didn't exist before. And I don't think his name is really Ray Price. I think he's a big old faker and not even a doctor."

Claudie of course couldn't argue with her about that. She thought a moment. "It's not unusual for a 'spiritual guru' to take a different name. And something you'll understand more when you get older is that people believe a lot of crazy shit. Sorry, stuff. It's a waste of time telling them that they're being silly. They won't thank you for it—believe me."

Maddie stood up and slammed her laptop shut again. "Sure, be just like the rest of them. I'm not some silly little girl that should just keep her mouth shut. I have just as much right as a grown-up to find out the truth."

"I know that, honey. I'm trying to tell you to let your father figure this out on his own. Show him some respect. He's smart enough to do this. It will be hard enough when he finds out, but if you're the one shining a light on this, it could humiliate him. Don't you see?"

Maddie gave a reluctant nod and picked up her laptop. At the door she stopped and looked back at Claudie. "You believe me don't you? You didn't defend Chrystal. You know what's going on?"

Claudie looked down at the table. She was afraid to give Maddie the validation she was seeking but she didn't want the girl to think she was betraying her. God, what a tangled mess this was.

"Maddie, if I do a little digging on Dr. Ray will you leave it alone for a while? Grit your teeth and not let Chrystal and her mom get to you? Can you do that?"

Maddie bounced a little on her toes, trying to decide. "How long?"

"I don't know. I'll do my best and if he's a fake I'll make

sure everyone knows about it. That way no one gets hurt."

"Except Chrystal. If she gets hurt it's her own fault."

Claudie nodded and Maddie said, "Agreed."

Oh God, what have I just done, Claudie thought. She didn't even have her computer here. At least she knew where to start. She had Dr. Ray's real name. She doubted he had been that discreet over the years that she wouldn't be able to find him. Thirty years ago she hadn't really cared. Now she would pick up the trail of her ex-husband. She would finally find out what she had dodged when he walked out. She had a feeling it was a very big bullet.

Sam came over on Christmas Eve and gave her a present that he had chosen himself. She could tell by the wrapping that he had done that himself also. She fed him cookies and he watched eagerly as she unwrapped it. It was a woolen hat with earflaps and ties in the most kaleidoscopic jumble of colors she had ever seen. It was a perfect fit. She had already tucked presents for all of them under their tree. She had found something for everybody at the bookstore, although Chrystal was a bit of a stretch. She had finally settled on a new age CD because if she was having a fling with Ray she might as well get used to it.

On Christmas day the Walkers piled into their car for dinner at Grandma's. Elaine didn't let anyone call her Grandma, of course. And she had bought the entire meal fully cooked from the local Kroger's. Claudie thought about going out,

Black Butte Resort was doing a holiday dinner, but she finally opted to stay home and watch *It's a Wonderful Life*. She cried and then made a big bowl of mashed potatoes with roasted garlic. With a good red wine she was content.

Corrine had a list from the county of every remodeling permit taken out in the last six months. It was a long list. Since the housing crash, people were staying put and, instead of trading up, they were redoing their kitchens, baths, basements, and garages. It was taking her a long time to sift through it. The weather was not cooperating either. In all the years she had lived in Central Oregon she had never learned how to drive well in the snow. She never remembered whether you were supposed to turn into the skid or the opposite. After scaring herself a couple of times she gave it up.

She'd hoped that Frank would take her around; living in Wisconsin for so long he should have been an ace by now. But he kept putting her off, saying he was too busy at the bookstore. It was better than him hanging around the house moping after that snooty wife of his, but otherwise he was useless and getting on her nerves. He kept taking control of the remote and making fun of the TV she liked. She didn't need to be mocked by her baby brother. She was just about ready to ship him over to TJ's house. See how he liked living in an RV for a change.

She was saving some of the houses that were way out in the woods for the spring when the roads were better. She needed someone to help her in town. She kept getting lost and forgetting what places she had already checked out. She needed a better system.

Coming out of Liz's one Saturday she noticed that Sonia's light was on in her little storefront. She had always felt a certain distant kinship with Sonia. People made fun of both of them. She admired how Sonia seemed oblivious to it. Corrine always tried to act like she was clueless too but she couldn't help lashing out when the snickers and snide remarks became too much. She never gave a fuck if she had friends so if she offended people she was firm in her belief that they deserved it.

She had never been into Sonia's place. The lighting was low with several candles placed about the small reception area. Crystals hung on ribbons in the windows and little bottles of herbal oils were sitting on a shelf. Some strange music was playing from small speakers. It was kind of nice, relaxing. The air smelled woodsy and spicy, and Corrine's body started to unclench for the first time in months. The doorway to the rear was hung with long strands of beads although Corrine could see an actual door behind them.

"Halloooo?"

The door opened and Sonia stepped through the beads and stood looking at her silently for a full minute. Corrine stared back. Now that she was here she almost felt silly. Why did she think that Sonia would be interested in helping her? She probably thought she was crazy like the rest of them.

"You are troubled." Sonia's voice was modulated to a low register. It was soothing like the music.

"Yes. Something bad is going to happen and no one will believe me."

"Come; let's see what the spirits can tell us."

Chapter Eleven

Claudie was dreaming, one of those lucid dreams where she knew she was dreaming, which was good because she sure as hell didn't want to still be married to Ray. They had hiked to the top of a mountain and he was pulling all this food out of his backpack: steaks and fingerling potatoes and fresh asparagus. Then he started a fire and began cooking everything on a barbeque, one of those heavy iron ones with an attached smoker. But he hadn't brought any wine; he just pulled a big joint out of his pocket and lit up, and he knew she didn't like to smoke so she was really pissed at him and just then an eagle swept down and snatched the steak and Ray started barking really high and loud. This was when Claudie woke up because the barking was really high and loud and right outside her bedroom window.

Thoroughly awake now, she got up and looked out. Mrs. Fowler's black pug mix was hopping around on the snow and ice. Why he was doing this outside her window and not Mrs. Fowler's was a mystery; she looked over to Mrs. Fowler's windows, which were dark, and waited to see if a light would come on. The barking was becoming more desperate. There wasn't a lot of fur on the little thing and it was probably freezing.

Claudie grabbed her robe and went to the door and opened it. The little black dog shot in like a bad omen and started racing around the small room. The yipping at close range registered on a decibel equivalent to front row seats at a Lady Gaga concert. Claudie considered throwing a blanket over it. Anything to make it shut up. She ended up sitting in her chair with the throw over her legs and the dog took one last spin around the room and then hopped into her lap.

He sat there facing her. His yipping reduced to a heavy snorting kind of breathing. He was trembling and she could feel he was as cold as a witch's tit, so she folded the throw over him and against her better judgment wrapped her arms around him. After a few minutes he stopped trembling but the snorty breathing continued; she suspected it was because of the smashed up nose that breeders had inflicted on him.

What to do? She could keep him overnight or take him

home, bang on the door, and wake Mrs. Fowler from her slumber of the dead. The self-righteous pounding appealed to her. After all, why should she be the only one with her sleep ruined?

Setting the dog on the couch, she pulled on her warm boots and shouldered on her heavy coat. The new woolen stocking cap added just the right insouciant touch. She hugged the dog tight to her chest and opened the door to a surge of cold air. Tramping across the street she thought she heard a faint banging. It got louder as she reached the door and gave the doorbell one long punch. The echoes of the bell faded away and she couldn't hear the thumping anymore. The house was silent and repeated assaults on the doorbell didn't change the stillness. Chilled and resigned, Claudie returned home. She was stuck with an overnight guest.

Inside the still house Marty and his new girlfriend Brianna, still connected doggie style, let the curtain slip back in place and resumed the vigorous rutting that was making Mrs. Fowler's headboard bang against the wall with such resonance. They were not in the least interested in why an old woman had been banging on the door. They were each happy that the person at the door had not been wearing a blue uniform.

Back in her apartment Claudie put the little dog down and wondered if she would be able to go back to sleep. The dog didn't appear to be ready to settle down. He was skipping like a mad thing from one object on the floor to another. She wondered if he was hungry; she still had a little sausage she could give him. She dug around in the refrigerator and took a small covered plate out, but stepping back she felt something soft under foot. The dog yelped and scurried away but then instantly came back. He craned his little head up, watching the plate with avid attention as she uncovered it and then cut up small pieces. He whined. He could smell it now and when she put a plate down for him he had inhaled the sausage before she could even straighten up. Smiling, she was about to cut up more for him when she remembered that her last dog Bear loved sausage but the memory also triggered the recollection of eau-de-dog farts. No more for you, bud.

The room was chilly so she decided to go back to bed and try to sleep. She wrapped the dog up in the blanket and tucked him in a corner of the couch. He was out tripping over her feet before she could shut the bedroom door. He leaped on her bed and immediately curled up beside her pillow.

"I don't think so. Move over, you little turd." Claudie shoved him over and climbed in; he cuddled up next to her shoulder and promptly fell asleep. In the quiet room his breathing sounded somewhere between a snore and the slurping sound when you pull a boot out of muck. It sounded like someone plunging a toilet, it was like … she was obsessing and she was never going to get to sleep. She turned the light back on and picked up her book.

The next morning Claudie was exhausted and cranky. Her one attempt at displacing the little dog by locking him out in the living room had just set off a torrent of yelps. Re-admitting him to the bedroom was easier than listening to his forlorn whining. The dog again went to sleep, wheezing loudly, and Claudie put dog breeders on her list of people worthy of damnation, if there was indeed a hell.

Strong tea in hand, Claudie looked across the street at the quiet house. It occurred to her that she had not seen Mrs. Fowler for some time. The son had come and gone, usually leaving late in the day and coming home some time after Claudie had retired. She made some scrambled eggs, enough to feed the dog also, and read the morning paper. She threw the dog out to do his business and half expected him to scoot home. After circling her car twice he finally lifted a leg and peed on one of her tires. He trotted back to her door and scratched expectantly. Inside again he followed her around as if connected by a short bungee cord and, when she sat, the little black thing did its best to wiggle into her lap. Claudie was mystified by the apparent devotion; she thought dogs were supposed to tell if you didn't like them.

After her shower, the one place the dog didn't try to oc-cupy with her, she dressed to run to the store. The dog was going home even if she had to sit in her car laying on the horn till someone came to the door. The worthless son had to be in there; his truck was parked in the driveway. She started the car to warm it and then carried the dog to his right-ful house. She repeated her onslaught on the doorbell and within a couple of minutes the son opened the inner door and stared at her through the storm door. He was bare-chested but Claudie was relieved that a saggy pair of sweat pants covered his nether regions.

"Your dog." She raised the dog and waved it in front of his quizzical face.

Comprehension slowly slid across his face and he finally opened the door and extended a large hairy hand. Claudie plopped the little black dog squarely in that hand. Marty turned and tossed it towards a chair; like a black eight ball hitting the rail it bounced once and then skittered down the hallway to the bedrooms. Claudie's eyes followed it begrudgingly, relieved that it appeared okay; she could see a woman in an oversized tee shirt do a little jig as it sailed past her legs.

"Sorry about that. The little wart gets out whenever I open the door." He was about to close the door when Claudie stopped him.

"I'm sure your mother was worried sick. How is she? I haven't seen her for a while."

"Oh, she's fine. Her sister's husband's got cancer and she's gone down to help out. She couldn't take the dog. My aunt's allergic. Well, thanks again." The door closed and Claudie was left with the horrifying and amusing notion of Mrs. Fowler being anybody's idea of an angel of mercy.

Chapter Twelve

"I t's for you." TJ backed away from the door and gave his father a look that would have skinned a cat, even one that was alive and objecting to the process. Frank rose from his marijuana-induced reverie and went to the door where he found a diminutive, in height only, young woman who was encased in a white down jacket that, because of her advanced pregnancy, looked rather like a snowball.

"Frankie." It was all she could say before erupting in tears. Cascades of tears ran down her cheeks and chin, and dribbled onto her white jacket. It was fortunate for the distressed young woman that the torrent of water blurred her vision and obscured the expression on Frank's face. It could only be described as aghast with a slight—no, large—sheen of panic. He roused himself enough to reach out and pull the poor girl into the RV and out of the cold. She buried her face into his chest and clung to him as the cataract of tears rapidly drenched his flannel shirt.

He looked over her head at his son who was pulling on his boots and shrugging on his coat. TJ stepped up to him and stood for a moment looking into his father's eyes; it was a look that Frank remembered from TJ's teenage years—a contempt devoid of pity. All parents recognized the look and prayed for the day when their offspring would once again look at them as if they were human. Frank grasped the fact that whatever advancement he had made since TJ's teenage years was long gone and he had now collapsed into a pathetic pile of parental failure.

"You are blocking the door."

Frank stepped away, the girl shuffling with him. Her head was still suctioned to his chest.

"TJ, I'll fix this. You don't need to worry."

The door slammed and Frank stood with the consequences of his actions standing damply in his arms. He had an absurd desire to call Marion and ask for advice. She would have known what to do, but of course her likely piece of advice would be along the lines of slashing his dick off and frying it while he bled to death.

TJ was speed-dialing Peter as he drove away. He should never have allowed his father to move in. But Aunt Corrine had had a meltdown and Frank had run for cover to his son's place. The man seemed incapable of living by himself. TJ needed mature advice from someone who could talk him down from patricide.

Peter answered and agreed to meet with TJ at Neil's Tavern shortly. He was dropping off the sad schmuck who had taken that last bend from Mt. Bachelor about twenty miles faster than the recommended speed. Even SUVs can spin out on icy packed snow, but he was lucky; he wasn't hurt except for the ding on his insurance and what sounded like a steep deductible. But since he was staying at Six Firs, Peter was fairly sure he could afford it.

The schmuck was too immersed in his own misery to think about tipping when Peter left him off but Peter had picked up a nice one from a woman earlier so he felt flush enough to afford a good microbrew with TJ. He glanced at the time and parked his tow-truck off in a corner of the parking lot. It was just at the beginning of Chrystal's shift and she might not be too busy for a quick hello. He entered through the bar and glanced into the dining room. It was nearly empty of diners and he didn't see Chrystal. The bar, though, had started to fill up with guests and a few locals who liked the higher-end version of happy hour.

The only waitress he recognized was Desi Arnold, a sweet girl who had somehow spent more time in detention than any other girl in her class. She was very suggestible; if anyone suggested something a little dicey Desi was their go-to girl.

He tagged her and after a surprised exchange asked her to let Chrystal know he was out front.

"I don't think Chrystal is working tonight. She's pretty much only doing the weekends now. Business slowed up real bad after the holidays. I thought she was doing some work for that guy, you know the spiritual one, Ray something or other. He's renting Mr. Cooper's condo while he's down in Tucson." Desi glanced over to the bar where the bartender was glaring at her with four cocktails lined up in front of him. "I've got to go. I sure hope they can start hiring again at the school. You were my favorite detention monitor." Desi hurried away, oblivious of the damage she had just inflicted.

Peter left and stood outside trying to remember where Harold Cooper had lived. The former math teacher had never been a favorite of his and he had only been to his place once, back when his first wife had been alive. His phone rang. It was TJ and he let it go to voicemail. Then he climbed into the truck and headed to Neil's Tavern. Maybe listening to TJ's woes would keep his mind from imploding. Maybe he would forget how his life had completely turned to shit. Maybe he would just get blotto.

TJ dropped off a very inebriated Peter at his house and drove home. It was a rare role reversal. Peter had sat quietly listening to TJ recite the sorry history of his pathetic father and it wasn't until the bill came that he realized that Peter had downed about twice as many pints as he had. TJ suspected that there was a marital explanation for it but he was relieved that he hadn't been called on to provide sympathy. Besides the fact that his own plate was full, he had always felt that Chrystal was a mistake. The hot sex would never make up for the manipulative personality. Even he knew that much.

He drove up to a silent and dark RV and let himself in. The door to his little bedroom was closed and, when he tried, it was locked. Just like his father. He climbed into the top bunk bed in the second sleeping area and fell into a deep resentful sleep.

At the Walker's, Claudie had draped a throw over Peter who had not even tried to negotiate the stairs and had elected to collapse on the white sofa. She had come over to sit earlier, until one of the parents showed up. It had become part of her routine and she used the time to work on the laptop.

Her investigation was coming along slowly. She had discovered that after Ray deserted her he had spent the first ten years or so wandering around the Southwest. He would pop up near some ashram or commune and then drift off to another. Seeking the meaning of life, the universe, whatever. Then he disappeared for several years and it was only when she found a divorce record for him and a woman in Southern California that she picked up the track again. It appeared to have been an exceptionally acrimonious divorce because of California's law about splitting assets acquired during the marriage. He had maintained that he had contributed greatly to her herbal supplement business and she maintained that he hadn't lifted a finger. She lost the debate and he walked away with a pile of cash.

She closed the laptop and then checked upstairs and found Sam and the black dog entwined and asleep. She was happy to leave the little turd there. Sam had been slowly appropriating the dog and apparently Chrystal had been too distracted to notice.

Downstairs she turned off all but a light in the kitchen and then, remembering her sweater, tiptoed into the living room to retrieve it. Before she could withdraw she heard Peter stir.

"Chrystal?" He lay with one arm draped over his face.

"No, it's Claudie. I was just checking in on the kids."

"Oh. You do that often?"

"Off and on." Claudie had no intention of telling him how often Chrystal had begged her to watch the kids.

"That's nice of you."

"Well, good night."

"Claudie?"

She paused in the doorway.

"Why'd you try to kill yourself? What was so bad that you didn't want to go on?"

That was a conversation she wasn't expecting. She didn't know what had knocked Peter so far off track this evening but he was obviously in the philosophical stage of inebriation—the stage where the big questions are explored; but usually in such a shambling fashion that they were rarely remembered the next morning. But she had always hoped to avoid talking about her near-fatal decision.

"I had a friend."

"He died?"

"She. After her husband deserted her she came to live with me. She was diagnosed with Alzheimer's a couple of years ago. It progressed fast. Last summer I couldn't take care of her anymore and she went into a care facility. It was like I had signed her death warrant. She died within a month. I couldn't bear the guilt."

"It wasn't your fault, you know."

"I know, but it was hard." Claudie laughed ruefully. "And then my cat died. It's such a cliché but I really miss her too."

Peter shifted, ready to fall asleep. "What was the name of your cat?"

"Mitten. She was a selfish little monster but I loved her."

"It's hard to love monsters."

"May I ask you something? While we're baring our hearts?"

Peter lowered his arm and looked at her.

"You've got a wonderful family, Peter. The kids are great. But what I don't understand is Chrystal. She doesn't seem … I don't know … the family type. Why'd you two get together?"

Peter gave a soft rueful laugh. "You know I taught children for over ten years. You'd think I'd know how to raise my own. But I was so afraid of screwing it up after Helen died." There was a long pause and Claudie thought he'd fallen asleep. Then, "I met Chrystal when I was going to grief counseling. She wasn't in the group. She knew someone who was and that person set us up. She was so sympathetic and the kids really liked her at first. Especially Sam. He was so young and he missed his mom. I just wanted to make my family whole again."

Claudie didn't know what to say to that but it wasn't necessary. Peter had drifted off. He wouldn't remember anything the next day. Not of their conversation at least. She let herself out the back door and hurried to her own bed.

The word for the week was *pernicious*.

Chapter Thirteen

Sonia normally reserved Sunday for a day of silent contemplation. Weather permitting, she would go out to the forest and allow the energy of the universe flow into her body and revive the damage inflicted on her soul by the material world. In winter she confined herself to the spiritual womb that she had built in her back office. With a fire crackling flames of energy and warmth, she would sit on her small couch and channel the spirits that swarmed around her.

But the energy flow had been badly disrupted by that stupid Corrine Bales; she finally gave it up and rolled a small joint. She didn't like to fall back on the herbal pathways to the ether but she needed to calm her nerves. She was astounded when Corrine had wandered into her shop. Although she had endeavored for years to keep the two sides of her existence separate she was sure that Corrine had breached this duality. But after a few minutes she realized that Corrine never really looked into her face. It was like Corrine was watching the world through a film running on the insides of her eyeballs.

Corrine was filtering the world now with the murder plot she had ranted about in Sonia's hospital office. She had made no connection with Sonia and the officious Mrs. Boyle of Sonia's normal life. And Sonia had not been able to dismiss Corrine so easily. Something was telling her there was more to it than the ravings of an obsessive compulsive. In her weekend incarnation she dealt with many cosmic disturbances and truth be told there was something very wrong going on in Sisters. She could feel it in the air. And it seemed to center on that dratted Claudette O'Brien and Chrystal Walker. Corrine hadn't focused yet on that duo. Weekday Sonia, the level-headed Mrs. Boyle, was inclined to stay far away from Corrine's madness. Sonia on the other hand felt it was her duty to explore the matter further. After all, a woman's life could be in danger. Besides, it was slow in the winter and she didn't have a lot to do to keep her busy.

She put on her bright purple coat, wrapped a long orange wool scarf around her neck, and went out to start her car to warm it up. She drove slowly; it was a frigid overcast day and looked like more snow was coming. She wanted to take

Corrine to two places to suss out the vibes. She wanted to see if Corrine could pick up anything on her own and she needed a control case. She knew that one of her customers had converted her garage recently and it was on Corrine's list. They would go there first and check it out. Then on to the Walker's and Mrs. Fowler's houses.

Corrine practically leaped out of the car when Sonia pulled up in front of the first house. She stood for a moment looking around and Sonia climbed out into the cold.

"You go look into that garage and I'll see what I can un-earth over here."

Corrine started walking carefully up the icy path to a small blue house. Sonia watched for a moment and then crossed the street. She could hear soothing music coming from the garage so she walked over to the door and peered through the glass window. She didn't see what Corrine was up to.

Corrine knocked on the front door but no one answered. She was sure someone was inside because she could hear a radio on in the background. There was a mail slot in the door and she bent and opened it.

"Halloooo?"

This was really very awkward and it hurt her back. She tried to see into the house but could only see a throw rug at the foot of the door. Suddenly the door opened and there was a pair of feet in leather slippers; she nearly toppled over into the man's legs.

Recovering herself with a noticeable lack of dignity, Corrine asked, "Can I speak to the lady of the house? I'm sorry to bother you but I need to speak to your wife." She pronounced this while she was trying to rubberneck into the house.

"Corrine? You know my wife died." The man said this with a gravity that Corrine immediately interpreted as recent grief.

"Sonia," she turned back to the street. "We're too late! She's died." Corrine was anguished at this development.

Sonia hurried over from her inspection of her customer's garage. As far as she was able to see, the garage had been remodeled into a small gym studio. There were three women inside doing downward-facing dog and Sonia hoped that they had not seen her peeping in at them. Those were three enormous asses jutting up. Sonia joined Corrine at the neighbor's door. Corrine was flopping her hands in agitation and the man looked like he was frozen in the doorway.

"Corrine, honey. No one's died. This is Nathan, the bookstore owner."

"He said his wife died. Oh the poor man. To lose a loved one over a garage." Sonia thought Corrine was going to start hyperventilating and she tried to calm her by putting her arm around her shoulders. Corrine shrugged her off. She didn't like to be touched.

"Corrine! Nathan's wife died five years ago. She's not the one."

Nathan shook his head in agreement while Sonia repeated

her statement a couple more times before it broke through Corrine's hysteria.

"Oh my God, thank God. I'm so relieved." She smiled in a wavering way at Nathan who decided in the turnaround from grief to joy at his wife's death that Corrine was behaving in a most unseemly fashion. He'd had enough and he was cold so, with a withering look at both the unhinged women, he closed the door and went back inside, the door firmly closed.

The two women climbed back into Sonia's green Subaru and sat for a few minutes to let the heater warm them up.

"Okay dear. That was a little unfortunate. Perhaps we should be a little subtler next time? Take a few moments to feel the vibrations emanating from the ether." Corrine ignored Sonia and unfolded the map that she had made of the possible sites of misdeeds. There was just one more in the general area and Sonia had said it would be the last stop of the day. They drove off, both women privately thinking that teaming up had been a mistake.

Claudie was at the sink washing vegetables for dinner, staring out at her apartment and what little she could see of the house across the street. Then she thought about Mrs. Fowler and wondered when she would return from her trip. Surely her sister had taken all the mercy she could stand by now and was anxious for Mrs. Fowler to spread her benevolence in another direction. The only people she saw coming and going were Marty and his two friends, and the straggly haired girl who seemed to live there now. Claudie knew in her bones that Mrs. Fowler would not approve of that arrangement. It would frost her real deep.

Claudie noticed the accumulation of dog turds dotting the thin covering of snow on Mrs. Fowler's lawn. She had trained Sam to always take the dog across the street to do his business. She sure as hell wasn't going to pick up dog poop. Sam had become a very conscientious dog owner and walked the dog a little both before and after school. He was going to be very unhappy when Mrs. Fowler came back to claim Pooh. It was fortunate that Chrystal hadn't noticed the presence of the dog. Sam had been very careful about keeping him out of sight when Chrystal was home, which wasn't much. She knew Chrystal was too busy banging Ray and side-stepping the curiosity of her mother and the dawning suspicions of Peter. Busy, busy, busy was our Chrystal.

She noticed a green car drive by slowly and then a few minutes later the same dinged-up green car pulled to a stop in front of Mrs. Fowler's house. Two women sat inside but she couldn't see them clearly. Then her view was blocked by Peter's tow-truck pulling into the driveway. He kept such odd hours; it was the nature of towing, she guessed. Nothing, nothing … then a little snow and ice and *bam*. Weekends were especially busy. She thought briefly of slipping back to her place but he came in by the back door. He started slightly when he saw her at the sink.

"Claudie, I hope that Chrystal hasn't been asking you to fill in for her too much. I'm sure you didn't plan on cooking for a family as part of the bargain." He wiped his feet on the rug by the door and stood looking around distractedly.

"No, don't worry. I promised Maddie that I would teach her some basic cooking lessons. I was just preparing some of the vegetables for when she gets back from music lessons. Chrystal said she had to go in to work early."

"Yeah, right."

Claudie surmised by the tone of Peter's voice that he wasn't buying Chrystal's excuses anymore. "Well, I'll get out of your hair." She wiped her hands on a towel and slipped on her sweater.

Peter held the door for her and she went back to her apartment. The dog had been sleeping but now was pirouetting in circles around her feet. He needed out. Grudgingly she shrugged on her coat and the wool hat and opened the door. On the doorstep was an older woman, her hand raised as if to knock.

"Can I help you?"

Corrine looked not at Claudie but past her into her apartment. She took a minute to answer, which was annoying.

"Are you looking for someone in particular?"

The sharp tone in Claudie's voice pierced Corrine's concentration and her gaze shifted to Claudie's face.

"Who are you?"

Corrine's question came out a little shrilly and just increased Claudie's annoyance. The little dog had been sniffing around Corrine's ankles but now decided that this strange person was perhaps a danger and started barking resoundingly. Both women looked down as Corrine swiped a foot in the dog's direction.

"Hey, don't kick my dog. Who the hell do you think you are? You need to leave now. Get!"

For a second the little dog thought Claudie was talking to him but quickly interpreted the hostility as directed towards the stranger. He increased his yapping and even made a couple feints at Corrine's ankles. Claudie was stepping forward to force the woman away from her doorstep.

Corrine backed away, something she had rarely did, but she didn't want Sonia to see that she had caused another brouhaha. Fortunately Peter's tow truck blocked Sonia's view and when Corrine scuttled back across the street Sonia was just returning from reconnoitering the old farmhouse.

"That's it, I know it." Corrine was breathless with excitement.

Sonia was freezing and wasn't going to stand outside the car discussing it. What she needed was some quiet to try to feel what the spirits were trying to tell her. She hadn't chanced that Claudie would recognize her so she had sent Corrine to check out the garage. She already knew what Corrine would find. She just wanted to know if anything would trigger more of Corrine's memory of the plot she heard in the hospital. Corrine was definitely agitated; unfortunately it kept the ether churned and muddy and she needed time to think. Sonia climbed in behind the wheel and Corrine scrambled in beside her.

"There's an old woman living there and it's definitely been remodeled into an apartment. Did you talk to anyone in the farmhouse?" Corrine was grinning and chortling. She wasn't crazy. She had heard that woman plotting.

"A young woman answered the door but she said she doesn't live there. Her boyfriend's mother owns it and she's on vacation. There's a lot of bad energy in that house. I'm not sure whether to believe her. She wouldn't say anything else. There was a man in the background and he told her to close the door." Sonia sat lost in thought. Corrine was craning to look up at the farmhouse but didn't notice that the farmhouse was looking back at her.

"What are those old biddies doing? Are they friends of your mother's?" Brianna was peeking through a crack in the drapes.

"My mother doesn't have any friends that I know of. Probably just a couple of women from church wondering where she's been." Marty stood slightly behind Brianna looking at the green car.

At that moment Gordon's truck came barreling down the street just as Peter started to back out of the driveway. Gordon laid on the horn and swerved past the tow-truck, coming to a screeching stop alongside Marty's truck beside the house.

Peter straightened out his truck and paused, watching Gordon as he started to haul a large box out of the back of his truck. Peter shook his head and then went on, one problem at a time.

Gordon muscled the large box to the ground and then went to the side of the house to retrieve the dolly. He noticed the green car parked in front as he maneuvered the box onto the cart. He could see two women inside it just sitting there watching him. They gave him the creeps. One looked just like his grandmother, the old bitch, and it was hard to peg the other. There was something sprouting off the side of her head and it made her look deformed. He twisted his face into a contorted snarl and he could see the flurry of reaction in the car. It was very gratifying. Whenever he'd made a face at his grandmother his father had always gone off and smacked him.

He trundled the box towards the barn. Marty came out the back and they walked together.

"Those two out front, are they your new girlfriends? If they're the jealous type I could take Brianna off your hands."

"Fuck you. Don't know who they are and I don't care. They were looking for my mom. Probably from her church."

Gordon gave a nervous look back and then a quick glance at Marty who didn't seem perturbed about the incident. Gordon started to get an uneasy sensation in his stomach. They were close to cooking their second batch. The first one had not gone well and they had been forced to start over from scratch. None of them would have given Walter White a run for his money. If this batch wasn't good then they would have to find a new source of pseudoephedrine. Jason was already whining about not wanting to take the risk.

Jesus Fucking Christ, these two losers were really beginning to try his patience. He'd tried to explain that those who took the biggest investment risk were the ones most likely to gain the biggest reward. Jason had twisted his wise economic advice and pointed out that it was important to spread the risk. Jason had stolen the initial batch of pseudoephedrine and Marty was supplying the location—at great personal risk if his probation officer got nosey. He'd had the nerve to ask what had Gordon risked so far?

That's when the partnership almost came apart because Gordon was quick to point out that he had relied on their supposed competence to produce the meth. If they were caught because they were fucking idiots then he would go to jail just like them. Marty had taken umbrage and took a swing. They were in the barn tumbling around and Jason was screaming at them to stop. He was also jumping up and down on the wood panel covering the old well and, with a snap back into reality, Gordon froze and took a hit on the shoulder but he didn't swing back. He started pumping his arm, pointing frantically at Jason's feet.

"Get off the fucking well, Jason."

Marty spun around with a puzzled look and Jason stood there on the wood like he was frightened to move an inch. "Yeah, meat head. I'm not fishing you out if you break it and fall in."

Gordon and Jason exchanged a silent brainwave on the wisdom of leaving the well intact. Multiple bodies would do no one any good.

Out front the green car pulled away. Sonia drove them to Monte's Take Five; they both needed a stiff drink and Sonia needed to relax. The bar was dark and overly warm from the sizzling fire at the end of the room. They sat near the front where cool air crept in from the edges of the door. Corrine continued to babble on oblivious to the fact that their work was only just begun. Fortunately the gin and tonic seemed to quiet her down.

Sonia could begin to sort out the conflicting auras she had experienced at Mrs. Fowler's. Perhaps Mrs. Fowler was on vacation and in no immediate danger. It would give them time. But, there had been something very odd in the atmosphere in that house and it wasn't just the marijuana smoke she could smell through the open door. They would have to go back so she could get another reading.

But not when the men were there. Sonia and Corrine were going to have to stake out the house and do a little snooping when no one was home. Sonia didn't know when she would have time to do it. She didn't trust Corrine to be on her own. Perhaps she would take a little time off. She was interrupted in her train of thought when the door opened and a little too much cold air swept over their table. The couple who entered paused in the door like they were judging the place; all the time cold air blasted into the bar.

"Coming or going folks? The air outside is a little nippy—want to shut the door?" The barman's voice indicated he didn't much care whether they came or went.

The tall older man gave the woman a nudge and pulled the door closed behind them. He stood for a moment longer and then guided her with a hand on her back to a corner table. Sonia had a good look at him when he sat and a glimpse of the woman as she twisted around to shrug off her coat. It was that real estate woman, MJ something. Sonia had been disappointed that the real estate crash had not wiped her out but apparently she had plenty of reserves from her divorce. That poor schmuck, her ex; MJ had taken all the cash and liquid assets and he was left with an equestrian ranch half full of horses that people weren't paying their boarding fees for. The big house in Bend was three years behind in property taxes and Sonia had heard rumors that the IRS was auditing the ranch.

And there was MJ like shit didn't stick to her shoes with a new fish, rich of course, and then Sonia gasped. She knew who the older man was and her heart did a little pitter-patter. It was Dr. Ray. She knew he had been flitting in and out of town. It was very hush hush but she intuited that he was looking for a new spiritual home. It couldn't be possible that he would pick their humble little town. All thoughts of Mrs. Fowler flew out of her head and she ordered another gin and tonic for Corrine to keep her nattering down.

MJ must be guiding him around to look at properties. But that was all wrong. First of all MJ's bad karma would distort his ability to thoroughly assess the suitability of a site's vibrations. Secondly Sonia herself was the one who knew the areas around Sisters that had the best spiritual auras. She had led over twenty retreats with people seeking the path to enlightenment. She of course was not anywhere near the level of Dr. Ray but she was the best person she knew of to help him in his quest.

She was lost in thought when the door opened and TJ walked through the door and made a beeline to his aunt. With the two gin and tonics in her, she was mellow enough to accept his offer to drive her home. TJ was rather curt with her, she thought, when he suggested that she let him or his father know when she was going to take off with Corrine. For heaven's sake, she was a grown woman. Crazy maybe but she had always been that.

She nursed her Irish coffee and watched Dr. Ray and MJ. They had started with martinis before ordering, so they were on their second drinks when the food arrived. Sonia was shocked when she saw the humongous hamburger and nest of fries set down in front of Dr. Ray. MJ of course was having a spinach salad although she wasn't beyond sneaking a few fries from Dr. Ray's plate. There was a sense of familiarity in the way she took them—not the way a stranger might beg for a couple but in the way a person who was very confident and, oh my god, intimate with the other person.

Sonia's mouth opened in a distressed O. There was no doubt about it. Those two were lovers. And now she could see how Dr. Ray had one of his legs pressed against—between!—MJ's knees. And he was downing that burger like he was starved. It was all so disgusting that Sonia finally had to leave. She wasn't sure how she was going to deal with the disillusion-ment. She felt her being shaken to the core. She needed to get back to her warm little cubbyhole and sit quietly with a cup of chamomile tea to soothe her nerves. Some aromatherapy too. They were always good when she felt like her world had suddenly upended itself.

Chapter Fourteen

nside the High Ponderosa Real Estate firm Chrystal was emptying her desk at the front of the office near the plate glass window. She was making the move during the lunch hour when everyone was out of the office. It was too humiliating and she'd already had to hide in the bathroom once while she was crying. She couldn't believe that, after all the time she had put into building the firm with MJ, because of one little dry spell she was being let go.

MJ had been so cold; it had been frightening. Mike and Jake had not produced a single closing since the fall either and she couldn't understand why she was being singled out. MJ had said that lately it had not appeared that Chrystal had been directing all her energy into her real estate business, which was true. Ray had taken up a lot of her time as she helped him organize his business plan.

MJ didn't seem impressed with the progress they had made hunting down the financing. She also hinted that contrary to Chrystal's belief that she could mine clients from the Six Firs, it was in fact detrimental to the firm to have one of its agents so publicly unable to make ends meet working as a glorified waitress. She used the word disgraceful. It was like she had slapped Chrystal. Then MJ had sailed out of the office with the explicit directive to have her things gone by the time MJ returned.

Chrystal had the last box sitting on the desk and looked around. She felt kind of broken inside. She had tried to call Ray but he wasn't picking up. She left him a series of messages but if he was meditating then it could be awhile. She thought briefly of going by his place but he'd been angry when she'd done it before. She had interrupted one of his mystical mediations just when trickster coyote was about to impart some of his deepest secrets. Ray had been distant and withdrawn for over a week. Chrystal didn't think she could take a week like that under her current state of distress. She took the box out to her car and headed home, hoping that Peter and the kids wouldn't be around to see her bring her things in like a whipped dog.

She was in luck. No one else was home and she was able to take all her boxes in unobserved. She set to putting things away so no one would notice. She had to slip some files under her bed and some of the books went under a pile of old bedding. The house was really filled to the gills. The loss of storage space when they had converted the garage had filled every closet and nook in the house. She thought briefly that she could take the time to do a real thorough reorganization of the house and get rid of a lot of the old crap that Peter had held on to. But she scrapped that idea almost immediately. Hell, she was not going to spend her time at home like some miserable housewife making everybody else's life orderly.

When she was finished she made herself a kale and beet smoothie. She stood looking out at the garage and thinking. One problem was that they weren't making any money on that space. Mrs. O'Brien had a pretty good deal and Chrystal was beginning to suspect that Claudie was not exactly destitute. Duh, the BMW may have been over ten years old but it was still a BMW. And she hadn't seen Mrs. Fowler for months. Maybe the old biddy had moved away and left the house to her scummy son. That unfortunately would be a win–lose situation. Marty's friends were every bit as scummy as he was and she had also noticed a slutty young woman coming and going. Chrystal swore she could see the meth sores on her face from across the street. God knows what they were cooking over there.

She went back to musing on the converted garage. She vaguely remembered saying something to Claudie about free rent for a year but maybe she could appeal to Claudie's sense of fairness. They had been good to her. Now they were in need. She would have to do it herself; she didn't even want Peter to know if she started charging rent. And, if Claudie objected then she would just have to find a way to make her miserable enough to leave on her own. She would have to figure out where Claudie was vulnerable. She wondered if she still had that social worker's name.

She looked around for her laptop and remembered that she had not packed it in any of the boxes from work. Damn and double damn. She didn't want to go back to the office and she especially didn't want to see MJ. But also particularly she did not want anyone at the office playing around with her laptop. She searched the kitchen and livingroom to no avail. Well, just get it over with. She pulled her coat on and went out to her car.

She drove by the office slowly to see who was inside. She could see in the back that MJ was at her desk and a man was sitting facing away from the window. She decided that she just couldn't face it so she drove on. Instead of going home she drove over to Six Firs and talked to the manager about getting more hours. It was one humiliation on top of another. The only job they had available was cocktail waitress on the dead nights of Monday through Thursday. It would be slow nights of being groped and propositioned for piddly tips. She swallowed her pride and said she would do it.

Peter was in the kitchen when she got home. She could hear him from the front door and he was laughing with Maddie and it sounded like Claudie. They all looked surprised when she came in and the laughter faded away. Jeez, she lived here too for God's sake. They were making dinner and she could smell a roast chicken in the oven. Her nostrils betrayed her; the chicken smelled delicious and she could pick out the scent of garlic and rosemary. With an inner shudder she made herself picture a filthy salmonella-covered naked bird. Better.

She picked up her copy of *Vogue* to take into the living-room and, lo and behold, there was her laptop. She could have sworn she had looked under everything. She glanced up and saw Peter staring at her. He had a funny expression on his face. He had been a little weird the last few days. Not his usual complacent self. In fact he'd been quite short with her about her last credit card bill. She'd always paid her own card but the last few months she'd needed to ask for a little help. One of the things she'd always liked about Peter was that he wasn't cheap. He'd never begrudged her before. She wondered what had changed.

Then she remembered how painful the day had been for her. Whatever was bothering Peter couldn't compare to the troubles she was dealing with. No one in this house appreciated what she was trying to do for them. She needed a break.

She poured a glass of white wine and sat to read the latest trends but, before she could get to what the hot new colors were going to be, she noticed something was not right about her beautiful white couch. There were black hairs in one corner. What the fuck, they hadn't let that stupid dog in here had they? She had been trying to be a big person about the dog; Sam clearly loved it, but on her new couch? She could hear them laughing again and she went to put a stop to that. It was her house too! They needed to respect that.

The second batch of meth was a success by way of not being a complete failure. The quality was in the low range but Gordon and Jason were sure they would be able to sell it. Gordon was going over the mountains to visit friends in Salem and Eugene. Jason was heading east to a contact he had in Baker City. They hoped to be back within a week. Marty's assigned task was scouting supplies for the next batch and doing more research on how to improve the purity of the meth.

Also on Marty's agenda was to search for his aunt's phone number. He couldn't find his mother's ancient green phone directory; perhaps she'd taken it with her. He couldn't re-member what city his aunt lived in so he had been unable to look her up on the Internet. He had gone through her bed-room and closet without any luck. He was going to search through some old boxes in the basement to see if there were any old letters or cards that might have the address. He wasn't too concerned yet. Gordon had told him a couple of times that his mom had called and had left messages about how badly his uncle was doing.

Peter was confounded. For two nights he parked outside of Harold Cooper's condo and waited for Chrystal to show up. He felt a little ridiculous especially since she never appeared. He wasn't sure what he would have done if she had. He was a little old to try to peer into windows. On the third night he drove by after Chrystal had left their house. Again there was no sign of her car. He turned back onto Main Street and kept an eye out. He hesitated at the Six Firs entrance and then swung the truck in and drove through the parking lot slowly. Tucked in the back was Chrystal's old Volvo. He sat for a few moments. It was possible that Desi had been mistaken. He didn't have the nerve to go in and check. He headed home but he still felt disquieted.

The spying had been beneath him, but the nights of waiting had given him time to think about his marriage. Some time last fall he felt things had started to go off track. Before, Chrystal seemed like an open book to him; an easy and enjoyable read. But over the last few months she had become distant. He had put it down to how hard she was working, and he felt bad about that. If he could get his job back at the high school then that could help get their lives back on track. He sighed ruefully. He knew that he was being overly optimistic. He was like a male Pollyanna.

"Okay, Maddie. Here's what I have so far. I've tracked him up to about 2002 then he disappears for about five years. I think he changed his name again. I can't find any records of Ray Price that go back further than 2007. Then all of a sudden he's owner of this supplement business that I think he stole from an ex-wife. He starts billing himself as some sort of transformational guru and begins giving seminars geared towards women wanting to change their lives. There's talk of scandals on a couple of blogs, which by the way I forbid you to read because it's stuff you shouldn't know till you're thirty or so."

Maddie rolled her eyes and made a mental note to do some digging on her own. They were sitting at the table in Claudie's apartment with the laptop between them. Also on the table was a package of Dr. Ray's organic rejuvenating powders.

The ingredients listed were several herbs with Chinese names, a smattering of Indian origin, and a few claimed to be grown from seed of recently discovered herbs in a remote Mayan valley. Claudie was sure it was all bullshit.

"It says here that this crap is made from herbs grown organically on small sustainable farms in Mendocino County. There are lots of small growers in Mendocino County although many of them are in what we call the underground economy."

"You mean marijuana?"

"Yes. I have a couple of friends down there I was thinking of calling and asking if they could dig up more information for me."

"How soon will you know?"

"I can't tell you, Maddie. I'm not a private investigator. You'll have to be patient. Nothing is happening now. We have time to turn up all the dirt we need to sink him."

"And Chrystal. We need to sink her too."

"That's not what we're doing here. If Ray goes down and he takes Chrystal with him then that's on her. What did I tell you before? You do not want to be the one that pulls the plug. That's my job. And after everybody learns who Dr. Ray really is then it's up to your father what he's willing to do about Chrystal."

"He wouldn't take her back would he?" Maddie's voice went up a register or two.

"I don't know, Maddie. I don't know. You need to trust your father. This is a very difficult time for him." Claudie looked into Maddie's closed-off face and realized how hard it was for a teenager to understand the adult world. Everything seemed so clear to her. She couldn't even begin to comprehend the confusing emotions that her father might be experiencing as he comes to terms with his wife's adultery.

"You better get back. I think I heard your father come home. Be kind to him, Maddie. He loves you very much."

She shrugged her shoulders, unsure of that statement. A

father who loved his kids wouldn't have saddled them with an evil bitch like Chrystal.

Chapter Fifteen

Chrystal was exhausted and she was making hardly any tips; minimum wage was not going to provide her with the spending money she needed. She'd already had two flaming arguments with the bartender and had finally realized that in this world he was the God and she was just shit. She had considered talking to her mother but then she'd have to admit to losing her real estate job and finally sinking so low as to sling drinks at a bar. It wouldn't be worth it.

Ray had finally returned her calls and she was meeting him after her shift. It was on her break when she gulped down a Dr. Ray's energy drink that she had her epiphany. She had been buying Dr. Ray products on the Internet and they were pricy. Why not convince Ray to let her start a distribution program, sort of like Mary Kay, and distribute the stuff that way? He had licensed a Canadian company to sell his stuff over the Internet but he had complained that they sold too many competing products and his revenue had gone down to a pittance. It would be a win-win for the both of them. She just knew it would be something that she could excel.

On the way to his condo she had visions of a new Lexus, in some signature color, maroon maybe. She would be the grand mistress of a health food empire; she could even branch out into some kind of new exercise program, maybe a Zumba-like routine mixed with some yoga. Revolutionary.

She had anticipated some reluctance on Ray's part so she was pleasantly surprised that he found the idea interesting. He wasn't alarmed at all that she wouldn't be working on the plans for his spiritual retreat. He was happy that she had something to focus her energies on and he didn't have any awkward questions about her real estate job. They were both tired and it was one of the first times that they had not had sex during their entire affair. Chrystal was too relieved to wonder why Ray was so exhausted.

She wasted no time in printing up brochures. She needed to canvass the main business area, post them in the local gyms, and head into Bend and even Portland. It was a lot of territory to cover. She hoped that she could guilt Claudie into helping her but that went nowhere, the old bitch. Well, it was best to start in town and leave some at the places she knew.

She started at Liz's, who was busy perming someone's hair so she didn't stay long; the chemical fumes are so cancerous. With a little hesitation she stepped into Sonia's. Basically she thought Sonia was a disgraceful quack with the fashion sense of that English actress—the one with the crazy hair in Harry Potter. She didn't know what Sonia thought about her; it never occurred to her that Sonia might think ill of her.

"Hi. Anyone here?" Sometimes when she was nervous her "hi" came out like a high-pitched bullet. The beads covering the door to the back room rustled and Sonia was standing there looking at her with an astonished face. Chrystal could hear someone talking excitedly back in the room.

"Sonia, hon, would it be okay if I left a few of these brochures for Dr. Ray's health products? I'm the new distributor and I want to get the word out." She held some brochures in her hands and looked around for a table to set them. It was strange; Sonia didn't say a word.

With a brittle "bye bye", she left some on a small table by the door and got the hell out of there. That woman was so bizarre.

Inside Corrine had rushed to the window and watched Chrystal walk down the sidewalk.

"It was her. I know it. That voice, I remember it exactly. It was so evil, so cheerful in a diabolical way."

Sonia, who still sometimes had small doubts about Corrine's conspiracy theory, was thunderstruck. Corrine didn't know who Chrystal was but she had identified her by her voice. Chrystal owned the converted garage across from the farmhouse. It spooked even her. And there were definitely bad vibes coming off that woman. Of course she had felt that for years.

Another interesting question. What was Chrystal's connection with Dr. Ray? From what Sonia had seen at the bar the other day, Dr. Ray was hiking up MJ Wien's skirt. Was the good doctor diddling both women? Sonia giggled. Maybe there was something in that green crap he peddled. It certainly kept him raring to go.

Chapter Sixteen

"Are you her father?" The nurse wasn't looking at him until he hesitated.

Frank was inclined to say yes to avoid some awkwardness but when he looked down into Gerlinda's blue eyes he knew that wouldn't fly. She definitely wasn't treating him like her father.

"No, I'm a friend. You know her pains are only seven minutes apart. How soon can she see a doctor?" He tried to keep the anxiety out of his voice. Gerlinda was nearly hyperventilating as it was. Although, if he could remember back, weren't women who were about to give birth supposed to breathe like that? He didn't think Gerlinda had participated in any pre-natal classes but maybe it was something that came natural.

The nurse handed him a clipboard with a bunch of forms and they went to a row of seats to begin to fill them out. It was hopeless. Gerlinda didn't have any of her insurance information and getting a health history out of her between her sharp groans was impossible. They brought a wheelchair around for her and he was left holding the mostly empty forms. He knew she was still on her father's policy but it seemed incredibly gauche to call and ask for the information. He took the coward's way out and gave Gerlinda's father's name to the nurse. He would know all the health history anyway.

He sat in the waiting room and wondered if TJ would be able to overcome his irritation at his father and come sit with him. It made him sad to think about the breakdown of the American Family.

"Can you believe it? He actually asked me to come down to the Bend hospital and sit with him. He couldn't imagine why I wouldn't want to be there for the birth of my new sister or brother. The dumb little twit never went in for any pre-natal stuff and she doesn't even know what she's having." TJ took a long swig of PBR. "On top of that my aunt Corrine and that batty Sonia Boyle are running all over town talking about some murder plot. They were heard talking in Liz's

Cut-n-Go about how weird it is that no one has heard anything from Mrs. Fowler since before Christmas. They think
Chrystal has done away with her. And Claudie is somehow
in on it. I'm the deputy sheriff in this town—do you know
how embarrassing it is to have my aunt raising all this fuss?"

"Who told you this? What has Mrs. Fowler got to do with
Chrystal?" Peter asked.

"Corrine thinks she heard your wife plotting to murder
Mrs. Fowler."

"What? Where would she have heard this?"

"Back when she was in the hospital. It turns out that she
was in the same room with Claudie when Chrystal came to
get her. Corrine heard something in her coma that has convinced her that they were plotting a murder because of that
garage of yours."

"Why didn't you say something? My God. I think I've even
seen them out in front of my house."

"I didn't want to tell you—it was just crazy talk. Apparently
she hallucinated while she was in her coma and when she
came out she was convinced that some women were plotting to kill another woman because of a garage conversion.
After trawling all over town she and Sonia have identified
the garage as the one that you and Chrystal had remodeled. Chrystal and Claudie supposedly were planning to kill
Mrs. Fowler because she objected to the conversion. Corrine
thinks that in fact Mrs. Fowler may already be dead because
she hasn't been seen at church or come in for her hair ap-

pointment since December."

"Can't you stop her? Should I get a restraining order or something?"

"I'm so sorry, Peter. I tried to distract her but she's like a speeding train, I can't control her. I've tried to get her back to the doctor, get a change in medication but she refuses to go. She thinks my dad and I want to commit her for her money."

Peter was sitting with his head in his hands. TJ got alarmed when he noticed Peter's shoulders jerking up and down. Then he lifted back his head and roared with laughter. Everyone in the bar turned to look but Peter couldn't stop for several minutes.

"This is just what I need now. You know, Chrystal may be up to some crazy shit but I don't think murder is one of them. She doesn't have the time between … Oh Christ." He stopped himself before he spilled the beans about his suspicions. Try as hard as he could, he had not completely laid them to rest. She was being open about her business with Dr. Ray. That of course could be the perfect cover. Like hiding in plain sight.

TJ stared down in his beer. Rumors about Chrystal's late night shenanigans had been circulating at Liz's Cut-n-Go too.

"Marty, Mrs. Fowler's son, said she was down in Arizona or somewhere visiting her sister. His uncle has cancer and Mrs. Fowler is helping out. I really don't think anything sinister is going on." Peter took a deep breath. What two crazy old women were fussing about really didn't concern him. His problems were much more complex than that. For a brief while he had thought the affair had cooled off. Chrystal was coming home at a decent hour and she seemed real engaged with the new business enterprise. He had thought perhaps she had just been so unhappy because the real estate business had still not rebounded and she was at a loss to keep herself busy.

She was a hustler; that was for sure. For most of January she had been in a continual bad mood. Now she spent all her time working on her new business. They hadn't had sex for over a month and she had totally neglected any household responsibilities. Maddie was in a tear because more had been asked of her. The raging female hormones in the house had him and Sam heading for cover at the first cross glance.

"I heard that the legislature was about to pass a big funding increase in the education bill. Do you think you'll get your job back next year?" TJ asked.

"Don't know. Maybe. Listen, I gotta run. I promised Maddie I'd help with some things around the house. See you later." He stood up and paused. "TJ, you know things are a little crazy around my house now." He paused again. "If you can keep your aunt away from us it would be greatly appreciated."

"Sure. Do my best."

Chapter Seventeen

Marty scrambled to pull his jockeys back up and grabbed a robe as Brianna's boney ass disappeared into Mrs. Fowler's bedroom. Outside he heard the doors slam on Jason's car and a couple of voices coming towards the door. Jason had forgotten to call before coming over and it was beginning to piss off Marty. Gordon and Jason were acting like they lived there too. Jason opened the front door without even knocking which was just another example of how they felt they owned the place. And he had someone with him.

Holy Jesus. He stood staring at the dark-haired man standing beside Jason. Everything about the guy was dark: his eyes, his thick moustache, and his stubble on the rest of his face. He was dressed in black pants, a black leather jacket, and black patent leather shoes. The only color was the heavy gold chain nestled among the curly black fur on his chest, an equally heavy-looking gold watch, and a gold ring as large as an unshelled walnut.

"Marty, this is Abe. He's the guy I was talking about from Baker City." Jason seemed oblivious that he had just dragged an Arab into Marty's house. Marty nodded at the guy, who eyed his robe and then looked around the room, real critical like. Abe? The guy looked more like a Mohamed than an Abe.

Before they could get any further in the introductions Gordon's truck came to an exhaust-fueled stop in front of the house. Great, a fucking party. He needed to get dressed. He left Jason and his friend in the livingroom and went downstairs to get some clothes out of the dryer. He had a tee shirt on and one leg in his pants when Gordon came rattling down the stairs.

"What the fuck is that upstairs?"

"Damned if I know."

"Jason! Could you come down for a minute?" Gordon waited with his back to Marty who was trying to zip up his freshly dried jeans. Too many pizzas lately. Brianna was good in the hay but not a Paula Deen in the kitchen. The house didn't even look that clean anymore.

"Wazzup?"

"Wazzup, you moron? What are you thinking with bringing a fucking Arab into the house?" Gordon was trying to keep his voice low but the vehemence of his feelings made his words resonate in the concrete basement.

"Abe's not an Arab. He's from Baker City. We went to school together."

"Christ, Lord fuck a duck. Marty tell him. If your mother found an Arab sitting in her livingroom she'd have a heart attack."

"Why's he here, Jason? You haven't talked to him about our little enterprise?"

"He's my distributor, Marty. He came back to see what our capacity is. He can move a lot of stuff if he thinks we have the ability."

"Oh, so Mr. Arab is going to pass judgment on us? Did it ever occur to you that we might want to check him out before you drag him here where we live?"

Gordon took a turn around the basement and then came up short when he discovered Abe the fucking Arab calmly watching him from the top of the stairs. The hairs on the back of his neck rose to attention. For a wild minute all he could think of was the Arab had them trapped in the basement.

"Gordon, is it? For your information my father's family came from Aleppo in Syria. We are Christian Arabs and while you wrap your head around that I need to inform you that Aleppo is one of the most ancient cities in the world.

And while my people were building empires your people were still picking lice out of each other's beards." Abe came down several steps and sat looking at the three men. They were clearly losers but then again all the men who supplied him with product were vermin. Whether they could be useful was another thing.

"I run a multi-million dollar corporation dealing in the distribution of illicit chemical substances that are regularly abused by your countrymen. That is their choice. It is my choice whether I think you morons can supply me with the product I need. I am here as a courtesy to my old friend Jason. He tells me that you have a perfect set up. I am here to see if that is indeed true. I must confess I wasn't overly impressed with the batch he brought me but it will probably do for the fools working in the fracking fields in North Dakota. Now, we can keep it at that level. You can make a meager living— enough for this shithole town. Or, if I have the confidence that you can improve with some guidance, then we can all make a lot more money. A lot more. Shall we see what's out in the barn, guys?" Without waiting for a reply Abe went back upstairs.

The three partners looked at each other and then shuffled towards the stairs.

"Okay, we can hear him out. But if he kneels down with his butt up in the air and starts to pray, I'm done. Do you hear me? If he thinks he's building a fucking empire on our backs he's got another think coming." Gordon's declaration gave him back a small sense of control.

Marty was uneasy because he knew that sooner or later his mom was going to come home and the whole enterprise would crash and burn. Plus she might kick him out of the house.

Jason was anxious because he really wanted to move out of his mother's house and head down to Arizona. He really hoped that Gordon wouldn't screw it up. But, to tell the truth, Abe kind of scared him now. It wasn't like high school. They stood together then because they were both picked on. One an Arab and the other made fun of because both parents were in jail. They used to call him the 'double birdy.' It never really made sense to him, but they didn't call him that because they liked him. All he really wanted was enough to get out of Dodge.

"Turn the heat back on. I can't feel my legs." Corrine was peering through a small pair of binoculars and occasionally rubbing the condensation off the car windows.

"Look hon, we haven't seen anything since those guys trooped into that barn. It's been almost an hour and I have to get back for a session. No one answered the door when I knocked so I don't think she's in there." Sonia started the car and without waiting for Corrine to agree she pulled out and headed back towards the main drag.

Claudie noticed the car leaving and shook her head. She had noticed it shortly after Gordon had come screaming up the road. There was a recipe for disaster brewing across the street. No one had seen Mrs. Fowler since December and she didn't like the look of Marty's friends. Whatever they were doing in the barn wasn't her concern but she wouldn't be surprised if they were turning it into some kind of grow room for marijuana. It was still a little cold and the barn would be drafty as hell but she wasn't about to give them any gardening tips.

The thing was she probably could. Her second husband tried to set up a small homegrown operation back in the '80s. They lived about twenty miles outside Portland on about five acres. He grew sensational weed but unfortunately he got ripped off before he made a dime. He finally decided to switch to financial planning and fared only marginally better. Somewhere in the process the marriage took a nosedive.

She looked up at the grey sky and wondered when spring would come. She was tired of the cold. Perhaps it was time to consider moving back over to the warm side of the mountains. Chrystal had been dropping less than subtle hints that she needed more space for her new business venture. She had tried to enlist Claudie in going around town with her brochures but Claudie declined. After that there had been a couple rather snarky remarks about how expensive Claudie's wine taste was; of course with hardly any living expense it was easy for some people to afford good wine. Claudie gave her a silent toast that night with a very nice Merlot from

Walla Walla.

She picked up her book bag and left the house. Pooh was sleeping on the recliner and Sam would be home soon to take him for a walk. Since Chrystal's little eruption the other week she had been careful about keeping him in her apartment. Not once had Marty come over to ask about the dog. Just as well—she wasn't overly fond of the little thing but she wouldn't want to think of him at the not-so-tender mercies of Marty and his straggly girlfriend.

Brianna told them that the two old biddies had been sitting in the green car for over an hour watching the place. It made Gordon nervous but he was already wired from the meeting with Abe.

"Call me next time they show up. I don't know what their problem is but it's going to get a whole lot bigger if they keep stalking us. We can't have some old crones poking their noses in our business. Not now." He paced nervously from the kitchen, where Brianna was heating up some macaroni and cheese with hot dogs, and back out to the livingroom window where he looked up and down the street.

Gordon's agitation had exhausted Marty who sat nursing a beer on the sofa. If his mother would at least call when he was around maybe he could go out and tell the old ladies that she was okay. The last thing they needed was for Gordon to go off the deep end and rough up some old women.

"You think that Arab was blowing smoke or do you think he can do all the things he talked about?" Gordon's way of saying 'Arab'—the way he drew out the A real long—was beginning to irritate Marty.

"Jason seems to think he can. If he can really supply some better equipment, that would sure help. I'm not too sure I like his idea of me going out to some secret lab and training with some yahoo. I think I've figured things out well enough."

"Yeah, but if we want that equipment you're going to need to step up to a whole new level of excellence, man. Wouldn't you like to cook like Walter what's-his-name from Breaking Bad? You don't want to be like that dumb ass guy—the one who shot the kid. He couldn't cook worth shit."

"Thanks for the vote of confidence, shithead."

Chapter Eighteen

TJ was sitting in his patrol car when Sonia pulled up in front of Corrine's house. He got out and stopped by Sonia's window. It was time to try to talk some sense into the two women. He was hoping to have better luck with Sonia than he'd had so far with his aunt. He was quickly disabused of that hope.

"I absolutely did *not* harass anyone. If two ladies can't take a little scenic drive around town, now that's what *I* call harassment, young man."

"It's winter, Sonia, and you keep driving up and down the same street. And you're going around town spreading rumors about Mrs. Walker and Mrs. O'Brien."

Corrine leaned across Sonia and yelled, "Hell! Big Deal. People in this town do that all the time. I don't see you harassing all the people who've spread rumors about me. Shit, if you arrested them they wouldn't all fit in the high school gymnasium." She shook off Sonia's restraining hand. Sonia was looking very pained by the whole encounter.

"I've talked to Mrs. Fowler's son and he says that she's down in Arizona visiting her sister. There's no murder plot. No one is in danger. You need to leave these people in peace."

"You can't stop us from driving around town anywhere we damn well please. There's something dodgy about that son and his friends. They're up to something. Did you check out what they're doing in that barn?"

"I have no reason to go snooping around their private property. I'd need probable cause and a warrant before I could do that. And if you two go trespassing on their property they could ask me to arrest you. Do you understand, Sonia? Aunt Corrine?"

Corrine just rolled her eyes, folded her arms across her chest, and sat with one of her knees bouncing up and down like a dog scratching fleas.

TJ left with the unhappy feeling that he had not made the unequivocal impression that he wanted. There wasn't much else he could do except patrol Peter's street a little more frequently. Unfortunately with the county layoffs his territory was twice as big as it was a few years ago. And with so many people out of work, well, they had that much more time and incentive to make trouble.

The hardest thing about dragging herself to the beauty salon was sitting in the chair with the cape tucked around her neck. Claudie was forced to sit and stare at her bare neck and the creeping—no, make that galloping—desolation of her skin. The turkey wattles below her chin made it hard to express to Liz how much she liked her new haircut. Finally Liz whisked the cape away and she could pull up her turtleneck sweater and hide the decay.

She paid and bundled herself into her coat. God, when will spring ever come? She stepped out into the bright sunshine and squinted as her eyes adjusted to the glare. It made her face look angry and Corrine, who was coming out of Sonia's place, paused and looked at her in fright. Claudie hardly noticed; she just nodded hello and started walking to her car. Before she made it twenty feet there was a hand on her arm jerking her part way around.

"I know what you're planning," Corrine hissed. "The police may sit back and do nothing but I'll stop you." Without a further word Corrine turned and marched back towards Sonia who was standing in the doorway. Sonia ducked back inside as soon as Claudie looked back.

Claudie was astounded; it was the same woman who had come up to her door last week. There were certainly more interesting characters in Sisters than she had imagined. She wondered if by chance it was TJ's aunt, the crazy one he had talked about. She walked towards Main Street; she wanted to pick up a book at the bookstore.

"Good morning, Frank. How's the baby?" Claudie could see Frank's brows squish together and his nose twitched.

"I didn't remember that they pooped so much. Is that something new? She's breastfeeding it. Marion couldn't for some reason. Jesus, in that little trailer it's like a stink bomb goes off every time she changes a diaper."

"I'm no expert but I'm pretty sure that frequency and smelliness of baby poop has remained constant over time. Perhaps the reason you don't remember TJ's so much is that you never helped your wife. Tell me, Frank, did you ever change a diaper or was that all just women's work?"

"Still haven't. It's not that I believe it's women's work, it's that I have a job and Gerlinda has hers. Now, are you here for that book I ordered for you?"

"Yes, and I want to look around."

Frank looked pointedly at the clock, "I'm going to be closing for lunch in a bit." He returned his attention to the laptop he had on the counter.

"Sure." Claudie could see that Frank still did not get the point of a bookstore was to sell books—the more the better. She looked over the science fiction section for a minute. She was tired of the mysteries that she had been reading. She found a Neal Stephenson book she hadn't read and brought it up to the counter.

On the counter was a pile of fliers; the colors and design reminded her of one of the old Beatles' albums—very psychedelic. Across the top in a large curved script was written *Frank's Amazing Web Designs*.

"What are you working on?"

"I'm starting a web design business. Nathan is coming back to the bookstore soon and I need something to keep me busy. And out of the house. I need to find a small office to rent so if you see anything let me know."

"Don't you think finding a place of your own with your family should come first?"

"Did TJ send you?"

"No, but I can just imagine that the RV is a little too small for all of you. It would be my version of hell."

Frank rang up her purchases without saying anything. She really didn't care if she had offended him. In fact she wondered if it was even possible to offend someone like him. She went out, headed down the block, and looked for a place to eat. On the corner was a new place for her—Monte's Take Five. Liz had recommended it; she said they had the best smoked turkey club she'd ever tasted. Plus good wine by the glass. She found a booth along the window and sat facing the main area. The waitress brought a menu over and she ordered a glass of red wine. She glanced at the menu but she knew she'd order the turkey club.

She sat sipping the wine and looking out at the nearly deserted Main Street when she caught Frank walking by. No, no, no. She waited and thought he had walked on to another restaurant but then the door opened and he came in. And as it happened he turned and looked right at her. It was one of those supremely awkward social moments and they were both undecided. Should they nod politely and then act like the other didn't exist, or smile insincerely and look like they would just love to have lunch with each other? Claudie smiled, cursing herself, and after the briefest hesitation Frank came over and asked if he could join her.

He ordered a glass of red wine and the turkey club and then Claudie tried to keep the conversation as noncontroversial as possible. Frank talked about a blog he had started; it was called "Late in the Day" and was about fatherhood late in life. Claudie actually thought it sounded interesting.

Thinking about his son TJ, she asked, "Frank, I have a mystery maybe you could help me with. This really odd woman came up to me outside of Liz's Cut-n-Go and, I don't know, she didn't threaten me so much, but she said the weirdest thing. 'I know what you're planning' or some such. Real dramatic. And then she kind of growled at me and said she'd stop me. She went into that psychic's place, Sonia's? The psychic with the beehive hairdo. They looked at me like I was some kind of murderer. TJ has talked about his crazy aunt Corrine. Would you have any idea what your sister is on about?"

Frank nearly spit out his wine with laughter. "I think I

know a little of what she's going on about. You have to understand that my sister has always been a little batty. When she was a teenager she went door-to-door for Goldwater. This was in Madison, Wisconsin. My parents were mortified. I used to think most of the Internet conspiracies I read about were started by her. I didn't have much contact with her over the years. She wouldn't come back to Wisconsin. She said she was afraid that the government might send a lightning storm to knock out her plane. She didn't want the death of all the other passengers on her conscience. She's a nut alright."

"She knocked on my door last week but she didn't ask for anyone. It was like she was looking around. And I swear I've seen her watching me. She and Sonia have been driving up and down my street. It's like they're casing the place out."

"Oh dear. She's been all over town looking for some garage where two women are plotting to kill a neighbor woman. She was in a coma for a couple of months and TJ says she had these strange coma dreams that she thinks are true. She's just out of touch with reality. Always has been. And you're living in a converted garage."

Click. Claudie asked, "Was she at the Bend Hospital in November?"

"I think so. TJ would know—you could ask him or Peter. Why?"

"Because I was in the hospital then and that's where Chrystal came to talk to me about her little garage remodeling that was in jeopardy. I think she may have overheard us talking.

Chrystal was not happy about Mrs. Fowler across the street because she was afraid she was going to contest the zoning change and they'd have to tear out the improvements. And I think Corrine was in the other bed still in a coma. She may have heard some of the conversation and wove it into some bizarre plot." *Double click*. "And even worse, Mrs. Fowler hasn't been seen since after Thanksgiving. Her son says she's visiting her sister in Arizona. But she didn't take her little dog and I had the distinct impression that she was quite attached to him. And no one in their sane mind would entrust an animal to the tender care of her son Marty."

"That's interesting. You know, I hear a lot of gossip at the bookstore. People talk to each other and forget that you're there. Two women came in looking for sympathy cards, which we don't carry, but they wandered around for a few minutes. They were looking for a card to send to Mrs. Fowler's sister, because her husband has cancer. I heard them talk about how Mrs. Fowler was angry with her sister because she was friends with the woman Mr. Fowler ran off with. In fact Mrs. Fowler accused her sister of knowing about the affair with his dental assistant and not saying anything to her. The women were surprised that Mrs. Fowler had gone down to help."

"Hmm. Marty said his uncle had cancer. Maybe she felt sorry for her sister. Christian forgiveness and all that. Her son's got some girlfriend practically living there. I'm sure his mother wouldn't appreciate that either. Plus Marty has some dicey looking friends and they are cooking something up in that old barn. It would be interesting to see if the electrical bill has suddenly skyrocketed. Maybe they're getting a head start on growing legal pot."

The waitress interrupted them with towering plates of turkey club sandwiches. They spent the next few minutes chewing and thinking.

"What were you in the hospital for? If you don't mind me asking." Frank noticed Claudie's eyes shift to the side. "I'm sorry, that's kind of personal. Never mind."

Claudie used a minute while she finished chewing a mouthful of turkey to decide how to answer. Several people already knew the story or at least thought they knew the story. But she didn't owe Frank an explanation either. She had thought TJ would've clued him in. Oh well, she was sitting across the table from a man who had so fucked up his life that he had lost his job and his wife, and was living in his son's RV with the teenage mother of his baby girl. What did she have to feel embarrassed about?

"Part of it's kind of silly. I drove to a campground and took some pills and drank some champagne. That's not the silly part. What I've pieced together is that I dropped the pills and while I was rummaging around for them I knocked a champagne bottle and the cork dislodged and plugged me on the head. Knocked me out cold. Peter found me while he was on a hunting trip and took me into Bend." She took a long swallow of wine and looked at Frank. She had his attention. "You may be wondering why I was trying to take pills with champagne."

Frank just raised his eyebrows.

"I had a temporary loss of hope. Hope in anything. Politics, the environment, friendships, you name it. My best friend just lost her battle with Alzheimer's and I no longer had any close friends. I had no one to talk to and I didn't have the energy to go out and find new friends. I felt a complete lack of joy. I … well that's it mostly. Does that shock you?"

"The Middle East shocks me. Global warming shocks me. The direction our country seems to be going shocks me. No Claudie, you don't shock me."

Claudie came close to bursting into tears. Frank had surprised her. Kindness—who would have thought? She was blinking rapidly; her vision was blurred and at first she didn't notice the man and woman who'd entered and found a table towards the rear of the restaurant. She blew her nose and it was then that she looked across the room directly into the eyes of Ray. He was seated with a woman, not Chrystal, and he showed no signs of recognizing her.

"Oh Christ. No, don't look." Frank had turned around to see what she had noticed.

"Who is it? The guy, isn't he the one who's supposedly going to build some kind of spiritual retreat?"

"So I've heard. He's also one of my ex-husbands." She was keeping her gaze down and slightly averted from the back of the room.

"Really? Does Chrystal know this?"

"What?"

"Isn't she supposed to be banging the guy?"

"How do you—?"

"I told you, I hear a lot in the bookstore."

"Remind me never to talk out loud in a bookstore ever again."

"TJ says that Peter's still in the dark. He seemed like a nice guy." Frank took another look back at Ray. "Isn't that Chrystal's real estate boss that your ex is with?"

"I'm not sure. I only met her once. They seem quite cozy."

"Chrystal came in the other day with a pile of those brochures of hers. She wants to become the Mary Kay of health food supplements. She's got big ideas. We talked about designing a website."

"Are you going to do it?"

"Sure, why not? The thing is that she wasn't sure she could afford it. I told her she couldn't *not* afford it. She'll be back. But I'm not dropping my price for her. If she wants to be some Internet tycoon she's going to have to pony up. I've got a baby to support—I need the money. Did I tell you that my ex-wife is holding up the divorce? She won't let me take money out of my retirement account until we come to a settlement." Frank launched into a tedious account of his troubles and Claudie quickly lost interest. He wasn't a total asshole; he had been kind about her 'accident', but his narcissism was trying after a while.

They finished their lunch and when they left she kept her

face down until just before she stepped out the door. She glanced back once and found Ray watching her with a slightly puzzled look on his face. She wondered if he could subtract the thirty years and forty pounds that separated her from what he might remember. She hoped not. She didn't want him to know there was someone in the area who knew who he really was. She wanted it to be a surprise when the truth was revealed.

"TJ, I have great news." Frank was sitting on the miniscule couch in the RV with his sleeping daughter in his arms. Gerlinda was taking a much-needed nap.

"You're moving out?" TJ left the door open despite the cold; the place smelled like baby poop, vomit, and who knew what else. If his father was trying to convince him never to breed he was doing a bang-up job of it.

TJ's eagerness was highly annoying to Frank. "No. I have a new job. The web design business I talked about—I just booked my first customer."

"No shit. Who?"

"Chrystal. She's starting a new business with that guy she's bonking, you know the 'guru', and she needs a website built."

"I can't believe you'd help her. Peter's my friend you know."

"Yet you don't tell him that she's screwing around on him."

"Yeah, well, that's a good way to lose a friend. Still, I

wouldn't do anything to help that guy. I have a hard time believing that he can pull off that development he's hawking. But you never know. The county's desperate for jobs and they've wanted another resort development like what's popping up in Deschutes county. Some people in Sisters were able to fight off the last one but I think they're too tired now. Too many people out of work. It wouldn't be very popular."

"Well, there's helping and there's helping. Giving Chrystal what she wants may not be what she bargained for."

TJ glanced at his father. He didn't like the glint in his father's eyes.

"I had lunch with Claudie the other day. I can't tell you everything she said—it was in confidence—but I have a question about a woman named Mrs. Fowler, the one your aunt's been going on about."

"What about her?"

"I pick up odds and ends at the bookstore. People gossip. It's been noticed by more people than your aunt that Mrs. Fowler has been gone an unusually long period of time. Some of them seem surprised that Mrs. Fowler has been so helpful and forgiving to a sister that she thinks betrayed her. From what I hear, Christian forgiveness isn't the church that Ina Fowler prays at. The gossip seems to be that she's more the hell-and-damnation kind of gal. With the bad blood those two had people doubt that she'd stay over two months. They think it even stranger that she'd leave Marty alone in her house. They say she's lucky he hasn't burned it down."

TJ mulled this over. Wouldn't it be crazy if Corrine for once in her life got it right? Not that Chrystal or Claudie did the old woman in, but something was not adding up. He really should go back and check on things. Unfortunately the county had him scheduled for a week of training in Salem. He would have to follow up when he got back. The most important thing was he was going to get away from his father and his shit for a whole week. This living situation was too much of a distraction from his duties. It had to change.

Marty had spent a grueling week in Eastern Oregon down some shitty ravine off all the main roads. He was pretty satisfied with himself though. He had learned tons of stuff. The equipment scared him at first. It was just like in *Breaking Bad*. They even had him wear a white suit and a respirator. But by the end of the week he, and most importantly Abe, thought he was competent enough to run a more sophisticated lab. The equipment was going to be delivered some night next week. With Gordon and Jason they should have it up and running by the end of February.

He was disappointed when he pulled into the drive that Brianna's car was not there. It was nearly midnight—a little late for her to be out. He walked through the living room noting the empty beer cans on the coffee table. He checked to make sure that they hadn't left rings on the wood and then went into the kitchen to find the sink was full of dirty dishes. Sheesh, the dishwasher was full of crusty dirty dishes. The whole house looked like crap. He went into his mother's bathroom and the sink was covered in smears of makeup and toothpaste. The bed was a twist of sheets, blankets, and fuck, there was a full ashtray on the bed stand. A shudder went through him thinking of what his mother would say if she walked in. He tried to call Brianna but it went to voicemail. It wasn't the homecoming he was hoping for. He heaved back onto the bed and stared at the ceiling. In a couple of minutes he was snoring deeply and oblivious when Brianna got out of Gordon's car and let herself into the house.

In the morning Brianna was all forlorn that she wasn't home earlier last night. Her mother had asked her to babysit her younger sisters. In fact her mother had been ill so much lately that Brianna had not been able to do much around the house. She was so sorry. Marty fleetingly wondered that if she was so busy away at her mother's then how could the house have gotten so dirty? But then he figured that Gordon and Jason had continued to abuse their guest privileges.

After a tumble in bed the two of them went to work. Marty took kitchen duty and Brianna started in the living room. She put some real effort into it. She even vacuumed under the furniture and that's when she found Mrs. Fowler's purse. She yelled out to Marty about where she should put it but he couldn't hear her over the vacuum. Instead of turning it off she just went down to Mrs. Fowler's bedroom and tossed it on the floor of the closet. She never noticed how heavy it was or even gave a thought to why Mrs. Fowler's purse was home but she wasn't. Soon the house would pass his mother's inspection and Marty could relax on that front at least. Now it was time to cook some meth.

Chapter Nineteen

On the phone with her mother Chrystal was laughing about what an old fool she thought Frank was. Knocking up a college girl was just plain stupid. But, he did know his way around the web design business even if he had to do the work in her kitchen to get away from the squalling baby. He had all these great innovative ideas for the website.

Elaine was helping her plan a huge launch party for when her website went live and she had booked the small ballroom at Six Firs. They were selecting the vegan appetizers to go with the Dr. Ray's assorted energy drinks that would be served but she couldn't decide on the decorations. Should she go with bright colors and pictures of dynamic healthy people going about energetic activities or subdued, more reflective colors and images of people seeking spiritual fulfillment in body and soul?

She needed Ray's advice but he had gone to Portland for a meeting with a venture capitalist firm. She needed to raise some capital of her own. The whole process was expensive and she had no cash left. Peter professed to having only enough to pay the bills and for food. He had been so cross lately and she knew that wasn't entirely true about the money. There was the kid's college savings fund that he contributed to every month. But she knew it was hopeless to try to get a loan out of that. She'd tried to tap it for the garage remodel and he'd nixed that idea real quick.

There had to be a way to access that money without causing a major fuss. Once she got going she would be able to pay it right back with interest. One thing about succeeding in business was you had to spend money to make money. And her new enterprise *Chrystal's Holistic Awakenings* was a sure thing. No doubt about it.

Frank was working in the kitchen when Chrystal was on the phone in the livingroom with her mother. Chrystal was one of those people who talked extra loud on their cell phones. Her comments about his personal life gave Frank the permission he needed to unleash his full anarchic energies on her project. In fact he was having a lot of fun designing Chrystal's website. She was open to all his most outrageous ideas. And Chrystal's own imagination, left untethered and unfettered, was a joy to observe. The sheer busyness of the site could give someone vertigo. The colors screamed off the screen. Chrystal kept adding steps to the checkout process like, "Since you bought this perhaps you'd like to add this to your cart?" She couldn't use the previous distributor's product descriptions so she spent hours every day toying with ever more convoluted ways to say the same things. Some of the verbiage was simply impenetrable. Frank wondered why she didn't have Peter review her writing. Perhaps things were not copasetic at home. Frank of course had no desire to clean up her prose.

Chrystal seemed unaware that Dr. Ray's affections were now directed to her former boss. That was going to sting when she found out. Frank wanted to be there. It was not noble; he admitted that. But it would help compensate for the latest trial. Chrystal had started bringing samples of various concoctions and had coaxed Frank into sampling them. He was surprised he hadn't vomited all over Chrystal's designer high heels.

Chrystal also wanted him to help her with her video presentation for the launch party. Now he could start to plot not only Chrystal's downfall but her erstwhile paramour's downfall too. The developer had to be crushed and Frank was being given the perfect tool to do it. It was like being given a gift.

Sonia looked at the caller ID and groaned. It was two in the morning and Corrine was calling. It was in fact the third time she had called and Sonia didn't know if she could take it anymore. She regretted her involvement in Corrine's obsession. It was wearing her out and her business was beginning to slide a little. Some of her customers were beginning to think she was as delusional as Corrine. And yet she couldn't ignore the evidence. Mrs. Fowler seemed to be missing, something shady was going on in that barn, and sitting in the middle of all this was that snotty Chrystal and that enigma Claudie O'Brien. With a sigh she picked up her phone.

"Sonia, you need to come now. Something's happening." Corrine was breathing heavily and her voice had gone up to a range that drilled Sonia's head back into the pillow. Ouch.

"Calm down, Corrine. Where are you?"

"I'm down the street from Mrs. Fowler's. There's a huge truck that just pulled in and backed up to that old barn. Something's up. You need to come witness this."

"Corrine, you know that TJ told you to stay away from there. If something bad is going down then you should call 911 and tell the police."

"911 is a joke. I think they've blocked my calls. They never answer."

"Corrine, it's two in the morning. Maybe they're helping someone else. They can't block your calls. That's illegal, I'm sure." Sonia thought for a moment. She could certainly sympathize with the 911 responders if they would like to ignore Corrine's incessant calling. Still.

"Sonia, even if they answer they aren't going to send anyone in time. There's maybe only one state police officer on duty at night for the entire county. I need you to come and corroborate what I'm seeing."

"I can't. I took a pill to help me sleep. I can't drive. Why don't you take a picture of them with your phone?"

"I'll come get you. I'm leaving right now."

"No Corrine. Don't. I'm too sleepy to be of any help. You should just go home and go to bed. You can tell TJ about what you witnessed tomorrow. Please, Corrine. Go home." With firmness, Sonia clicked her phone off. This had all gotten out of hand. Please Goddess, let this end.

Corrine was left cussing into her phone. Why did everybody turn out to be such weak willie-nillies? If she had to do it all by herself, then fine. Now if she could figure out how to use the fucking camera on the phone.

Across the street Marty was chatting with the driver as he lowered the back lift gate. The dude had gang tattoos all over his neck and hands. He grunted every time Marty said something; he was more gruntative than talkative. Marty turned back to the several boxes on the lift gate. This was a lot of stuff. Gordon and Jason were maneuvering a large box onto a dolly to move it into the barn. Temperatures had risen and the ground had thawed and it was soft and muddy. It was slow going and Gordon was already complaining. Nothing unusual there.

He caught a small flash of blue out towards the street and he walked back down the driveway. Balls, there was an old lady standing at the end of the driveway taking a picture of the truck. Shit fuck. He started to shout but stopped himself in time. That driver looked pretty tough. Majorly tough. Marty wanted the old lady to go away but he was afraid of the driver getting involved and being a little rough with the old biddy.

Marty started walking towards the woman and she started chirping in a high-pitched voice, took one more picture, and then scampered back to her car. It was a different car than what he'd seen before. Still, he knew it was probably Corrine Bales. Brianna had told him that she was running around town talking about some murder plot.

He stood there as it drove off and wondered what to do. Abe would not be happy if he thought the equipment and cook site might be compromised. Then it occurred to him that no one ever took Corrine seriously. She might even provide a distraction. He figured the cops knew it would look pretty silly following up on one of her crazy ideas. She would need a whole lot more proof than a photo of a truck to get a cop to listen to her. He went back to help move the boxes into the barn. He would figure out later what to do if she became more of a nuisance.

Chapter Twenty

Peter could hardly get in the front door. There were stacks of boxes lining the hallway. The livingroom was also cluttered with boxes. They were all labeled *Dr. Ray's Miracle Potions*. He wouldn't have been surprised if the labels read *Distributed by Hogwarts*. This was getting out of hand. In the kitchen he found Chrystal hunched over her laptop and talking on her phone. No sign of the kids. He went back out to the hallway and looked at the boxes. One of them had a shipping label taped behind some clear plastic. He pried the tape off and unfolded the shipping invoice. The total charge took his breath away. They didn't have that kind of money. What was Chrystal thinking?

He went back into the kitchen and stood with the papers in his hand, waiting for Chrystal to notice him. He eventually walked over and set the invoice down on her laptop. She stared at it for a moment, glanced at him, and then ended her call.

"Peter, I know what you're thinking, but I need to have inventory on hand for my launch party. By the end of next week all these boxes will be gone. Aren't you excited for me?"

"I'm happy that you're happy. Just one thing—how are you paying for all this stuff? The invoice is marked paid. Where did the money come from?"

"Oh, I've had huge numbers of preorders. You'd be surprised."

"I'd be surprised if you had enough preorders to cover the cost of this shipment. There aren't that many whack jobs in Sisters. So again, where did you get the money? Another credit card you haven't told me about? I can't keep up with the payments on the cards we have already. Or did Dr. Ray pay for all this? Is your compensation of a more personal nature?" He paused and took a deep breath. He wasn't sure he was ready to get into that argument yet. "What are your plans if he can't get that 'spiritual retreat' off the ground?"

"I don't know what you mean by a more personal nature. And it's not true about the transformational center. He's working with some venture capitalists in Portland. And no, he didn't pay for this inventory. This is all my business."

"That he gets a cut of every time you sell this shit. Nice

little arrangement he's come up with. And let me tell you, no amount of venture capital is going to make his spiritual retreat get approval from the county. I just read an article in the Bend Express, Bitsy Jones has come out against it."

"Who's Bitsy Jones?"

"She's the state senator who has family property on the Metolius. She blocked the last development that got floated by the county and she'll block this one. The county guys shit in their drawers whenever she looks cross-eyed at them. Your spiritual guru is about to get his ass kicked."

A small frown formed on Chrystal's carefully made-up face. "You don't know everything, Peter Walker. Ray has made some powerful friends in this community. He can bring a lot of jobs to this town. Money still talks."

"Yes, and getting back to what started this conversation, where'd you get the money for those boxes?"

"From savings if you must know." She turned her back on him and stared at the white board on the refrigerator. The word of the week was *equivocator*. She had no idea what that meant. But now, when she thought about the words written over the last few months, she began to recognize a sinister pattern. Maddie was going to have to be taught a lesson when she had time to think about anything other than getting her business off the ground. She realized that Peter was still talking and she was running out of ways to deflect him.

"I repeat—you don't have any savings that I know of. Where was it? It wasn't in the bank where we have our checking and the kids' college savings. Oh my God. You didn't. Chrystal, look at me and tell me that you didn't get into their savings—did you?"

"No, I emphatically did not."

"If I call the bank what will they tell me?"

"That your silly kids' funds are still there safe and sound. If you must know I sold my ring."

"Your engagement ring? I'm sorry, sweetie, but that wouldn't pay for half the boxes of crap out there. What else?"

"The pearl necklace—only I just pawned that." Chrystal wouldn't look him in the eye.

"Maddie's pearl necklace? The one that was her mother's that we had in the safe deposit box?" Something in Peter's heart snapped.

"We can get it back, honey." Chrystal's voice was beginning to sound a little desperate. She had never heard Peter sound so angry.

"You bet we will. What else?"

"Your golf clubs. The generator. We weren't using that anyway."

"Anything else? Am I going to have to nail things down around here? Shit, Chrystal. I don't know. I just don't know about you anymore." He stood staring out the window for a few minutes; an icy cold fog was enveloping him. Chrystal let the silence lengthen. She really didn't have time or energy for this now. Her launch was only a week away and her focus needed to be on her business. Not on the death throes of this stupid marriage. Once she got this off the ground and Ray got the county approval, then it was goodbye sad-sack Peter and his pathetic offspring. Peter left the kitchen and she heard him go upstairs.

Marty pulled into the driveway and turned the truck off. It gave off one last smoky belch and died. It was loud enough to warn Brianna and Gordon to break off the fumbling grind they were doing in Mrs. Fowler's kitchen. Marty went directly to the barn with a sack and immediately turned around and went in the back door. Gordon was drinking a beer at the sink and he could hear Brianna vacuuming in the livingroom.

"What the hell, Gordon? I told you. You need to watch over that stuff all the time. This batch has to come out perfect. Abe expects us to be professional about this. Fuck knows what he'd do if we screw up his equipment. Dump the beer and go back out." Marty started to go find Brianna. He wanted to ask her if she'd seen the old lady again.

"Where you going?" Gordon sounded aggravated.

"I'm going to talk to my girlfriend if you don't mind." Gordon was really starting to bug Marty. And he didn't like him hanging around the house with Brianna when he wasn't home.

"Yeah, well, bring some sandwiches or something out when you're done." That sounded lame even to Gordon but he didn't want to say what he felt, which was "she ain't yours anymore, dude." He didn't want to spring that on Marty till the meth was cooked, sold, and the money was divided. He'd learned enough now that if Marty objected to the transfer of Brianna's favors then he and Brianna could go off some place and cook their own. He would have the capital to invest.

Brianna said she hadn't seen the old biddy but said she would keep on the lookout. Marty made some sandwiches and went out to the barn. It was awesome how things were progressing. He had a really good feeling about this batch. If they got good money out of this then he wouldn't worry so much about his mother coming home. There were plenty of old places further out of town that they could set up. He could get a new Dodge Ram pick-up and transporting the equipment and product would be easy. Maybe he would have to wait on the Dodge on this first batch. Abe's cut was higher on this one to compensate for the equipment and instruction.

He went to check things and everything looked good. The first batch should be ready to ship in a couple of days. Abe was coming to inspect it and soon he would be in the money.

Claudie discovered quite a few sites and blogs devoted to Dr. Ray's Rejuvenating Powders. Not all of them were complimentary. One in particular caught her eye. The blogger claimed to have worked at Dr. Ray's production plant in

Santa Rosa. If what he said was true, then she had Ray dead to rights. She left a comment and her phone number on the blog and waited for a reply. It didn't take long.

"Where are you calling from? It sounds like you're in Nashville or something." Claudie found herself shouting into her phone.

"No, I'm at Buck Owen's Crystal Palace in the San Joaquin Valley." The blogger had to shout into his phone to be heard over the background cacophony.

"Your blog was very interesting. I'm wondering if you have any proof you can show me?" Claudie strained to listen to the reply.

"Oh yeah. Tons. I took pictures and videos. Tell me, if I send these things to you, are you going to be able to nail the slime ball?"

"I hope so." She paused. "What, may I ask, did Ray do to make you so angry?"

"The guy's a huge rip off. The legit growers around here want to tar and feather him."

"But you, what's your beef?" All Claudie could hear for a minute was Buck Owens wailing in the background.

"He banged my girlfriend. Listen, I'll send what I got to you. Let me know if you take the bastard down."

Claudie hung up and began thinking about how she was going to spread the word about Ray's true background. She wanted to get it to the widest audience. It occurred to her that the upcoming launch event would be perfect. It would have the added bonus of saving people from wasting any more of their money on Ray's bogus powders. The downside was Chrystal. If she failed at her new enterprise then she would come scuttling back to Peter, and Maddie wouldn't be happy about that. Claudie realized that she couldn't take down Ray in a way that wouldn't also take down Chrystal, and there was no guarantee that bringing Chrystal down too would stop her from trying to twist Peter around her little finger again. This was going to be very dicey. Fortunately she had found a collaborator sitting right next door, working his devious heart out on Chrystal's website. They were natural allies and it was time to coordinate their plans.

Chrystal stared in her closet with disgust. Absolute junk. She needed something new, bold, stunning in fact, to convey the magnitude of her new enterprise. She didn't want to look like some wannabe from a dinky town in the middle of Oregon. And she didn't have the cash to bankroll a new wardrobe. But her mother did. And she was very anxious that her daughter should succeed in her venture. A little mother-daughter shopping trip to Portland would be just the trick.

Maybe she could catch Ray there. They had barely talked in the last week. She couldn't tell if his venture capital search was going well or not. He sounded stressed and his conversation was clipped. Maybe a visit with her chakras would put him in a better mood. It wouldn't hurt her either. Peter had moved into Sam's room and had hardly talked to her since the day the inventory had arrived.

He had retrieved the pearl necklace, she knew that, but it had not mollified him. If he didn't shake out of it she wasn't sure she wanted him at the launch party. Happy enthusiastic people were what she needed to pack the room. She had sent out over a hundred invitations and so far she was getting a good response. All was going according to plan. Thank God for her mom and Frank.

Chrystal and Elaine left early in the morning and arrived at the Nordstrom store in Portland shortly after it opened. They spent a couple of hours there and then headed to the Ann Taylor store. She still wasn't sure she had found the perfect outfit although Elaine was taken with a lilac suit at Nordstrom. She wasn't sure. She felt it might make her look too light and not substantial enough for a major business enterprise.

Before they stopped for lunch she called Ray to see if he could join them but it went straight to voicemail. Elaine was due for a cocktail and it was never wise to delay that imperative. They chose the Palm Court at the Benson and found a table by the street windows. The lobby restaurant was all old wood and brass and Chrystal fervently hoped that soon she would be able to afford little jaunts to Portland to stay in such luscious places. She people-watched as Portland's elite walked by. Her eyes didn't register the occasional homeless person. She could see down the street where many well-dressed people were coming and going at another luxury hotel, The Lucia. She wanted to stay at all of them. The Heathman, The Nines, The Riverplace—all of them. And in suites, not dinky rooms.

She sighed. It was within her reach; she could taste it. She took another sip of her Pinot Gris. Out the window she watched a taxi pull up to The Lucia's front entrance and a tall, elegant-looking woman disembarked. Chrystal squinted. The woman looked a lot like MJ. She grabbed her mother's reading glasses from the table but that only made her sight worse. Lowering the glasses she could see it was MJ and she was greeting a grey-haired man standing under the entrance canopy. The man's face was in shadow but she could tell it was a very warm greeting by the possessive hand the man put on MJ's lower back. Hmmm. MJ had always been secretive about her love life. Maybe she had a married lover here in Portland. The two lovers disappeared into the hotel lobby. Wouldn't it be fun to blow that out of the water? Throw a little mud on MJ's carefully crafted and pristine image. All things in their time. For now, she had to decide between a lilac or pearl-grey suit.

"Maddie, is Frank here?" Peter had found Frank's car in the driveway again. It was irritating that he didn't park on the street. He thought from what he could glean from Chrystal's phone calls with her mother that the launch presentation was complete. He'd hoped that he'd have Frank out of his hair. Whenever he found him in the kitchen Frank was drinking one of Peter's beers and with no encouragement he would begin to complain about TJ, his soon to be ex-wife, and the general vicissitudes of life. He was really a pretentious bore and Peter had little patience with him.

"Maddie?" No answer. The kitchen was deserted. Peter looked out the window and could see a light on in Claudie's window. He went out and he could see through the window in the door the tableau of Claudie, Frank, and Maddie sitting around a laptop. He tapped on the window and then opened the door. His entrance was like a shot of electricity as the co-conspirators straightened up and Frank hurriedly shut the laptop.

"Hi." He could see guilt on Maddie's face, consternation on Claudie's, and Frank just looked smug.

"Am I interrupting something?"

They all said "no" at the same time.

Back in the days when he was a vice-principal he dealt with teenagers who were equally recalcitrant about explaining the offense that had led them to his office. Back then he had a small portion of power over their lives, but he had no similar leverage with Claudie or Frank. Maddie had been a closed book to him since Christmas and he doubted she would crack.

"I see. Maddie, I was going to start dinner. Want to help?"

"Sure. Just give me a minute and I'll be right there."

Peter looked at the three of them. Claudie was examining her fingernails, Frank took another sip of one of Peter's beers, and Maddie looked away from him. Peter turned around and went back to his house. Whatever they were planning would come out eventually. He could only hope that Claudie's good sense would keep the other two from doing anything foolhardy.

Once the door closed behind him the three collaborators opened the laptop and reviewed the alternate presentation for Chrystal's launch party. They had each played a part. Claudie and Frank provided narration. Maddie had contributed research and back-up documents from Chrystal's email accounts. The emails were only to be used in the case that Chrystal tried to wiggle her way back into Peter's good graces. Maddie wasn't going to be at the presentation despite her protests, so Frank would be the one to reveal to Chrystal the futility of trying to crawl back into the marital bed. He said it would be a pleasure.

Peter and TJ carried the last two boxes of Dr. Ray's crap into the room that Chrystal had reserved for her launch party. Elaine was helping Chrystal put up a couple of banners and Frank was setting up the large screen TV and connecting it to Chrystal's laptop.

"Are you coming tonight?"

"Are there going to be any women?"

"Dozens from what Chrystal has said. Of course they all may be a little screwy. You should taste that shit she's selling. Supposed to keep you young and vigorous."

"Does it come in a beer flavor?"

"Nope."

"I'll pass. But I might come to scope out the women. I don't mind screwy. They tend to overlook my shortcomings."

Peter smiled. It was another couple of hours before the event would start and he wasn't interested in hanging around. He headed out the door and nearly bumped into Dr. Ray himself. The two men nodded and passed each other. Peter realized that he didn't even feel any heat or anger at the man anymore. He would do his duty by Chrystal and show up tonight, but that was that. He was going to talk to her about a separation. Now he needed to get home and fix the kids some dinner.

Frank had the flash drive for the alternate presentation and it was burning a hole in his pocket. He was anxious about downloading it to Chrystal's laptop. He hadn't taken the chance earlier because he was afraid that Chrystal would discover it before the Launch. He looked around the room.

Dr. Ray was talking to Chrystal in a corner and her mother had finally disappeared. The laptop sat on the podium in the front of the room. It took but a moment to download the new and improved presentation. The event was scheduled for seven. And if all went according to plan, the meltdown was scheduled for somewhere around seven thirty.

Chrystal was disappointed that Dr. Ray couldn't help her overcome her opening night jitters but he promised to be back at seven. With a final inspection, she headed to the suite her mother had reserved for them. She still had to decide between the lilac and the pearl grey. Her mother had insisted on buying both suits. Elaine was as anxious as her daughter for her to succeed. In the suite Chrystal looked with disapproval at the partial bottle of Sapphire gin that sat by Elaine's chair. The last thing she needed was for her mother to get crocked. She could hear her in the bathroom; she was taking a shower. She took the bottle and poured out half into the outer sink. She topped it off with tap water. If she had already had a couple she might not notice the difference. Now—lilac or grey?

She felt a little guilty when her mother came out and presented her with one last gift.

"I thought this would look sexier than that old black laptop of yours." Elaine pulled a shiny red Dell laptop out of a box and displayed it for her.

"I had one of the managers in the business office get it up

and running and he downloaded your presentation. I ran it through this morning and everything was perfect. You are going to be such a success, my darling. I'm so proud."

Chapter Twenty-One

"Jason, you dickwad. This is the third night in a row you've crapped out." Gordon was not happy. He hadn't gotten laid for a week. Marty was monopolizing all of Brianna's time and every time Jason couldn't do his shift it was Gordon who had to spend the night watching pressure gauges. He was sick of it.

"I've got the flu, Gordon. I come home from work and collapse. I don't have it in me to do a night shift. It's not like you have a day job."

"Fuck you. I'm helping pinhead Marty during the day too. He spends most of his time smoking dope and banging that chick."

"Work something out with him. I'm not coming over to-night." Jason hung up and pulled the covers over his head. He felt like dog shit. Let Gordon and Marty figure things out.

Gordon checked the gauges and then went outside to smoke. It was still warm from a sunny day but he knew the temperature would drop once the sun set. He wondered if Brianna had cooked anything decent for dinner. He headed for the house. He wanted a beer and if he was going to do a double shift he wasn't going to do it stone sober.

In the house the kitchen was empty and there were no signs of food prep. He stuck his head into the livingroom and it was empty too. Down the hall he could see the bedroom door ajar and hear a mattress wheezing rhythmically. Fucking Marty. And that bitch too.

He went back into the kitchen and opened some cupboards. Crackers, Kraft macaroni and cheese boxes, and some off-brand soup. He shut the doors and considered his options. A burger sounded good. He could run down to Jack's Tavern and score a beer and a burger. He would check on the barn first and then head off. Nothing was going to happen if he was only gone for thirty minutes or so. He glanced at his watch. It was nearly seven. He would be back by seven thirty or eight tops.

Corrine watched Gordon go. The house looked real quiet.

She hadn't seen anyone else since she parked about an hour ago. She had watched Peter and Claudie leave and there had been no sign of Chrystal for a couple of days. It felt like the right time to explore that barn. If she could just get some proof for TJ then he could come with a posse and take down these sleaze balls. And if that went well then she might get someone to listen to her about Chrystal and Mrs. Fowler.

It was dusk now and she slipped out of her car. She shivered; she was chilled from sitting in the car and she pulled her long coat close around her. She pulled her hat down low to cover her face. The ground was muddy and it was a slog to walk around the edges of the property so she could skirt the house. No lights on in the back either. Good. Now to see what those boys were up to.

Chapter Twenty-Two

Chrystal stood by the door in her lilac suit handing out brochures to people as they entered. She surveyed the crowd; it wasn't as full as she'd hoped. There were side tables with the different powders displayed and up front near the podium Elaine stood handing out samples. Frank was opposite her talking excitedly with Claudie. It was nice how seriously he was taking her launch. Dr. Ray was standing near the podium watching the crowd. Peter was sitting in the back with TJ and she noticed Claudie slip over to them and sit. Frank was walking back and forth behind Ray and she couldn't figure out why he was so nervous. She was the one who had the whole show resting on her shoulders. She was going to be a star.

"I need you to not ask too many questions, Peter." Claudie leaned in towards him. TJ was on her other side.

"What's up?"

"Frank and I have prepared a little surprise and we need you to distract Chrystal."

"Why would I do that?"

Claudie took a deep breath. She had very little time to choreograph this dance. "Okay, it's like this. I know Ray from way, way back."

"Really?" She had TJ's attention now.

"Yes. And none of the baloney he's fed Chrystal is true."

"That's hardly a surprise. So are you guys trying to expose him during Chrystal's presentation?"

"That's the idea."

"Just when I thought he was going to take Chrystal off my hands. She's always wanted to marry a big shot. I should help her, not hinder her."

"Except he can't marry her. He's already married."

"Damn. How do you know this?"

Claudie looked up towards the ceiling and then blurted out, "Because he's still legally married to me."

"Fucking no way." This was TJ. Peter was too stunned to say anything at first.

"He walked out on me thirty years ago and I had no way to find him to get a divorce. He's been marrying other women and swindling them out of their money for years. I think it's time to put a stop to it. Please, we don't have much time."

"Chrystal doesn't have any money, why her?"

"I think she's just been a means to an end. You'll know all of it if you can just get her away from that podium. We put a new presentation in her old laptop but she just showed up with a brand new one. Her mother gave her a shiny new red one and Frank has to download the new program on it. And, TJ, I need you to draw Ray over to Elaine by the refreshment table and get him talking about one of his damn powders." Claudie stood and looked down into Peter's doubtful eyes. "Do this for your children, Peter. Maddie is counting on you."

Peter stood up, "Emotional blackmail is beneath you, Claudie. But if you guys are going to expose the truth about this turkey then I'll do what I can." He walked over to Chrystal and began talking. He positioned his body so that she was facing away from the podium. She didn't look like she had much patience for this now.

TJ went over to where Elaine was handing out samples of a Dr. Ray concoction and, taking one, he turned towards Dr. Ray and asked him a question. Dr. Ray couldn't quite hear so he stepped over to them and TJ began asking about the properties of the drink he was choking down with a forced smile on his face.

Frank hesitated for an instant and then swooped over to the podium and slipped the flash drive in the new laptop. Chrystal tried to end her conversation with Peter but he held onto one of her hands and talked urgently about their relationship. If Chrystal wanted out then he wanted things clear before the shit hit the fan. There would be no going back when Dr. Ray got his ass handed back to him on a platter. Chrystal was furious at Peter for bringing this up now. Elaine had broken away from Dr. Ray and TJ and joined her daughter. Elaine made it unmistakable that further communication would be through Chrystal's lawyer.

Frank stepped away from the podium and gave Claudie a broad smile. She felt a sudden wash of relief and sat down. Peter sat next to her and sat with his arms crossed over his chest and a sardonic smile on his face as Chrystal went to the podium. It was seven thirty and the performance began.

They listened as Chrystal enthusiastically began her spiel: how she had discovered the Dr. Ray herbal powders and the incredible change they had made in her life. She avoided Peter's eyes. It was now time for the video portion of the presentation. It was going to be a smash; she just knew it. She stood off to the side next to Dr. Ray.

The video began with new age music and images of herbs and plants. Chrystal's voice was narrating. She spoke of the dangers of the typical Western diet and she extolled the virtues of a vegan lifestyle. She talked about the properties of various herbs and how they were blended into botanical elixirs by Dr. Ray. The video gave way to vistas of Redwood forests and people hiking in the mountains. The biography and history were the next parts but Chrystal's narrating voice suddenly gave way to another voice.

"Ray Barnes was born in Waterloo, Iowa. His mother, Cora, was an elementary teacher and a Baptist who had a firm aversion to alcohol. His father, who was also named Ray, was a butcher who died when Ray was very young. At least that's what he was told. The family rumor was that Ray senior tired of Cora's teetotalling ways. He found comfort with a barmaid in Cedar Falls and was never mentioned again.

"Ray grew up to be an introverted man interested in philosophy and the mysteries of drugs and sex. He dedicated himself to exploring all paths that led away from mundane commitments to family and wives, of which he has at least four, concurrently. His favorite quotation is from Carlos Castaneda, 'We hardly ever realize that we can cut anything out of our lives, anytime, in the blink of an eye.' End quote." The video continued to show smiling people gathered around a campfire in the desert.

Chrystal was panicked. This was not the presentation that they had previewed in the morning. And why was that woman's voice so familiar? A few people in the audience were whispering. She turned to Frank who whispered, "It's okay, I made a few changes. People like to hear about a sinner who turns his life around. Be patient."

The video continued. "The self-styled Dr. Ray, never having finished college, became a spiritual guru to a succession of women over the years. He has helped relieve them of the burden of existential angst and an excess of cash in their savings accounts. Another quotation from his favorite guru, Carlos Castaneda, 'Nobody knows who I am or what I do. Not even I.' He is currently working with a local real-estate woman to build a spiritual retreat outside of Sisters."

There was a picture of Ray and MJ in Monte's Take Five. She had her shoeless foot shamelessly ensconced in his crotch as he chomped down on a huge hamburger. The next picture showed them outside her car with Ray's hand up her shirt and his groin pressing her into the driver's door. Their mouths were firmly locked. Frank was very proud of these photos. He found his new camera phone quite remarkable.

Chrystal turned to Ray in horror. She felt the blood throbbing at her temples but he didn't even have the decency to look at her.

"Ray has been peddling his healthy powders for nearly a decade. They are supposed to be made from herbs and plants organically and sustainably grown in Northern California, India, and China. In fact, they are all grown outside of Santa Rosa downstream from a waste dump. The owner of the farm makes no effort to grow sustainably and chooses to use the same petroleum-based fertilizers so favored by Ray's fellow Mid-Westerners."

The video changed to a dry-looking field full of straggly weedy plants. Near the field was a large barrel with a yellow danger label on the side that read, "Pesticides are liberally used." Now the video changed to a view of a warehouse where a large pick-up was parked by a loading dock outside. A worker was standing in the bed of the truck on top of a pile of plant material. He was using a pitchfork to shovel the tangled mass into a bin. The picture switched to the inside where the bins were being emptied into something that looked like a large cement mixer.

"The custom blending of the herbs entails a thirty-minute tumble in a commercial soil blender. The pulverized result is then dumped on a conveyer belt and processed by workers in the next room. The only difference between the various potions is the slight bit of GMO-manufactured beet and kale to make the concoctions appear different. Needless to say, this is all allowable because of lax FDA enforcement." The video shifted back to images of Dr. Ray's magical potion packets.

"Bottoms up!" The video screen went blank.

What started as titters became a gentle roar of laughter. Someone started clapping. Chrystal turned to Ray; she sounded like a snake on fire as she screamed at him. Then out of nowhere she landed a right hook on him that she didn't know she had in her. Her mother, now completely sober, came up and grabbed her arm before she could inflict more damage and dragged her to the door. On the way they passed Peter, who could not force the big grin off his face.

"I blame you for this, Peter Walker. If you'd done your job as a provider none of this would have happened." They marched off.

Peter looked down on Claudie. "That was some nice narration there. How did you get all this stuff?"

Before she could answer, Ray walked by but stopped and looked intently at Claudie.

"I see you made it out of London all right. I wasn't sure before but I recognized the voice. You do all that by yourself?"

"No, I had a lot of help."

Ray looked at Peter and then back to Claudie. "Are we still married?"

"No, after a few years I got a divorce. Abandonment."

Ray nodded. He rubbed the left side of his face and looked back at the crowd and then walked out.

"I thought you said you were still married to him?"

"I embellished. I didn't have a lot of time to motivate you. What are you going to do about Chrystal?"

"She's got her mother. She'll be fine. She made it plain before this debacle that she had no plans on coming back home. She needs to get out of town though. This crowd will make it hard for her to show her face in public."

"Actually she may have to go farther than Bend." A young woman was standing by them with a big grin on her face. "My name's Selene. I'm a reporter from Bend. This is quite the story, and I got few juicy shots to boot. I don't think Chrystal or Ray will escape this easily." She sighed contentedly. "I've always believed that bad Karma gets you in the end. I've been covering Dr. Ray's efforts to build a spiritual center and I thought he just didn't smell right." She sat down on an empty chair and started texting her editor.

Claudie and Peter started to go. Peter looked around for

TJ but he was now deep in conversation with another young woman who was looking a little weepy about the whole turn of events.

"Let's go home and tell Maddie."

Claudie burst out laughing again. "I wonder what the word of the week will be now?"

Chapter Twenty-Three

"Who the hell is that?" Marty was at the kitchen sink getting a glass of water. Outside he caught a glimpse of a small figure going into the barn. The person was too short to be Gordon or Jason. "Damn." He only had a pair of undershorts on and he hurried back into this mother's bedroom for the rest of his clothes.

"Where the hell is my other shoe?" He bent down and felt along under the bed but no luck. He sat back on his haunches and then remembered that when he used one foot to pry the shoe off the other that it went flying and landed in the closet. He crawled over on his knees and groped around.

He found several pairs of his mother's shoes and tossed them aside. There on top of her purse he found the shoe. He picked it up and sat on the bed and put it on.

He frowned. Something was not right. He stepped over to the closet and picked up the purse. It was heavy. Not an empty purse—a full purse. He opened it and started pulling out some of the contents. There was her bottle of aspirin, a makeup bag, tissues, coupons for the grocery store, and in the bottom was her wallet. He opened the wallet and there were her driver's license, credit cards, and cash. Lots of cash; she liked to travel with a lot of cash. She didn't trust out-of-town ATMs.

Brianna heard his cry from the livingroom where she was rolling a joint.

"What is it, honey bear?" She stood in the bedroom door dressed only in an oversized tee shirt of his. Marty was sitting on the bed running his hands over a bunch of stuff from his mother's purse.

"I don't think my mom's at her sister's." He looked up angrily at Brianna and she stepped back in fear. "While I was gone, Gordon said my mom called a couple of times. Did you ever talk to her?"

"No Marty. I never. Gordon told me she called when I went to the grocery store, that's all. Why? What's happened?"

Marty charged past her and raced to the back door. He flung it open and ran towards the barn shouting for Gordon the entire time.

Inside Corrine Bales had satisfied her curiosity about what devilment the straggly men had been up to. She'd watched *Breaking Bad* and she knew what a meth lab looked like. She wasn't stupid. She was almost to the barn door when she heard Marty coming and she ducked down behind a barrel.

The barn door banged open and Marty stood in the entry looking wildly around for Gordon. The son-of-a-bitch was hiding. What the fuck had that asshole done with his mother?

He called Gordon's name one more time and then began to search, beginning with the side opposite where Corrine was crouched. She thought she could slip out while he was busy but, just as she started to stand, Gordon walked into the barn and stood watching Marty as he crept slowly along the far wall looking behind the equipment.

"It's okay, Marty. I checked on it before I left. You're being paranoid." Gordon started towards him and then stopped because there was something peculiar in the way Marty was looking at him.

"Where's my mom, Gordon? What did you do to her?"

Gordon had never heard such menace in Marty's voice. He took a step back.

"It wasn't me, Marty. Jason was supposed to fix that cover on the well. You know? She fell in. She came out here one day and Jason found the cover all caved in."

Marty roared and charged. The two men grappled and the next ten minutes were more a shoving match than a fight. Corrine knelt down with her arms wrapped around her knees and her eyes tightly shut, listening to the grunts and heavy breathing. Then things really got out of hand and they started banging into the equipment and barrels.

Brianna had pulled on a pair of jeans and shoes and was screaming in the doorway at them. Corrine heard a loud crash and then the pitch of Brianna's screams went up several decibels. Corrine could smell smoke. A sharp suffocating miasma enveloped her and she tried to stand and run for the door. She couldn't hear the men anymore and Brianna's screams had stopped. For an instant it was like all sound stopped and then there was a loud boom and she was flung out the door into the mud.

Peter heard and felt the explosion before they turned onto their street. The sky was orange behind Mrs. Fowler's house. He hastily pulled into the driveway and parked. They got out of the car and they could see the barn burning, and the flames raging in the darkness. There was an acrid smell in the air. The front door opened behind them and Maddie and Sam stood in the doorway.

"I don't like that smell." Claudie glanced back at the kids.

Peter turned and shouted, "Get back in the house. Close the door and shut all the windows." The kids backed up and the door shut.

"We should call 911."

"You do that. I'm calling TJ and the fire department directly." Peter stood by the car and watched the fire as his calls went through. Claudie couldn't abide the smell and retreated inside the house. Peter was about to follow her when he noticed Corrine's car parked half a block away. Damn that stupid old woman. He sprinted to the car to try to convince her to drive away. The car was empty. He looked at the house. Marty and his girlfriend were throwing bags into the pick-up and before Peter could shout at them about Corrine, Marty fired up the old truck and they swept down the street.

He stared at the house and then ran to the half-opened door. There was a good chance the house could catch fire also. He ran from room to room but there was no sign of the woman. He went to the back kitchen door and looked out. Between the barn and the house there was what looked like a body. It was lying face down in the muddy path. He opened the door and shrunk back a little at the heat and fumes. Then he ran out towards the woman lying in the mud.

He was lucky; the wind shifted and the flames and gases flowed back towards the empty field behind the barn. Corrine's coat was smoldering and he rolled her over and picked her up. He stumbled around to the front of the house and then over to his front yard. He could hear sirens over the roar of the fire. He set her down on the ground and opened her coat. She was still breathing but was unconscious.

The first fire truck raced to a halt in front of the house and firefighters tumbled out of the truck. Peter waved one of them over. The first responder did a quick assessment and then ran back to the truck for oxygen. TJ showed up and

Peter started telling him what he knew and witnessed. TJ told him to get back into his house away from the fumes and keep every window and door closed.

Peter went inside the house and joined Claudie and the kids at the front window. An ambulance arrived and carted off Corrine. TJ was going door to door on the street warning people to stay inside. The firefighters had all donned respirators and were putting most of their efforts into saving Mrs. Fowler's house. The wind stayed steady, blowing the smoke away from the street. The barn was a total loss and it would burn for another couple of hours.

Selene felt like she had hit a triple-header. She heard the explosion before driving out of the parking lot at the Six Firs Resort. She followed the fire trucks and parked way back. The Deputy explained that it was likely a meth lab explosion.

Claudie could smell something bad coming from Peter and she suggested he take a shower and let her wash his clothes immediately. The kids stayed glued to the front window like it was the best YouTube video they had ever watched. In the shower Peter noticed the burns on his arms when the hot water hit. He finished quickly and dressed. His arms were really painful now. Corrine's smoldering coat must have done the damage.

He came downstairs and showed Claudie his arms. She insisted he go to the hospital and he objected. The street was full of fire trucks and he wouldn't be able to drive his car out. Exasperated she looked out and spied TJ by his car. She opened the door and waved him over. TJ agreed with her but he was now blocked in too, but there was the reporter in a car down the block. Maybe she could help.

TJ and Peter walked to Selene's car and she was eager to be of assistance. A first-hand account of the fire and explosion plus the background information about the house and occupants. Home run.

It wasn't until morning that Jason heard his parents discussing the fire and learned that his Arizona plans were now on hold.

Marty and Brianna were halfway to Grant's Pass. She had a brother who lived out past Applegate where no one had seen a sheriff's deputy since the voters had nixed the last public safety levy. Marty only prayed that Abe didn't have any contacts out that way. He felt real bad about leaving his mom's body like that. He thought he should probably write and tell someone what happened. Maybe when he got around to it. He even wondered about the little black dog. Nothing in life panned out the way he planned.

The morning after the fire Claudie brought the kids along when she went to pick up Peter at the Bend hospital. When they learned that he might have breathed in gases from a meth lab explosion they insisted on keeping him overnight. Peter was dressed and waiting for them in his room. The reporter,

Selene, was with him taking more notes. The kids burst into the room and the reporting stopped. Selene joined Claudie who was standing outside watching the reunion. Sam and Maddie were excited because the newspaper had portrayed Peter as a hero for rescuing Corrine.

As they stood looking into the room Claudie heard the tat-tat-tat of high heels clicking down the corridor. She glanced back and saw Mrs. Boyle with her head buried in a file folder headed to the last room on the left. A nurse came up with a wheelchair and they all headed to the entrance. Selene asked Claudie about her role in the little play from the night before. She had several questions about Chrystal and wondered if now that her plans were in ruins if she would be going home. Claudie, off the record, told her that she didn't think Chrystal was going to be a part of Peter's life anymore. It didn't escape Claudie's notice that Selene had a small twinkle in her eye on hearing this.

Mrs. Boyle stood at the end of the bed looking down on the comatose form of Corrine. It felt like déjà vu all over again. She sat by the bed and tried to cast about for Corrine's aura but it was faint. Her crazy friend might be slowly dissipating into the ether. She hoped that she would find some peace at last. She felt real bad about how things had turned out. Corrine might not have been right about Chrystal and Claudie, but she was right about something being evil at the Fowler house. If she came out of this coma Mrs. Boyle hoped she didn't remember any crazy dreams. And she hoped that Corrine didn't remember how her alter ego Sonia had been involved. Sonia was hanging up her detective hat. All she wanted to do on the weekends was work with people with small everyday spiritual problems. She patted Corrine's hand and left.

Frank came later and signed the 'do not resuscitate' forms. It made him feel awful but to tell the truth he was amazed that the old battle-axe hadn't just died from a stroke. It was just like her to put this burden on him.

It was a week before TJ got the fire department report on the blaze. By that time he had reviewed the pictures he found on Corrine's phone. He talked to a friend in the State Police office and a certain truck was put under surveillance. It would be months before the State Police raided the ranch down the ravine outside of Baker City. Afterwards Abe had plenty of time to inform his jailers about the superior history of his family. They weren't impressed.

Corrine would have been so proud to find out that she had contributed to the downfall of the biggest and most foul drug ring in Oregon history.

Chapter Twenty-Four

Outside in the warm sun Claudie looked at the old farmhouse and wondered what would happen to it. The area where the barn had stood was a blackened heap of burned wood. Mrs. Fowler's car had been discovered in the forest but there was no sign of her or why she would have driven down an old logging road. They'd probably never know. Lucky for Sam and Pooh she didn't take her little black turd with her. The dog and Sam were inseparable now. It was about the only good thing to come out of the fiasco across the street.

She looked over to the house and she could see Maddie through the window reading a recipe in the cookbook that

Claudie had given her. She glanced up and waved Claudie to come in.

"What's up, cookie?"

"I need a consultation." In the weeks after Chrystal had jumped ship Claudie had impressed on Peter and the kids that she was more than willing to help guide them. But she wasn't going to be their housekeeper or minder. Maddie went on, "I want to make a cake and I need to know if I can substitute baking powder for baking soda. Do you know?"

"All I remember is that it's recipe for disaster. You've got your laptop, just Google it."

"I thought you knew all there was to know about cooking." She smiled mischievously at Claudie.

"You've found me out. Listen, Frank's helping me set up my blog and I need to connect my new laptop to your wireless router. Do you know the password?"

"MaddieandSam. Capitalize the names. Are you going to start your blog? Have you decided on a name?"

"I'm going to write my first one today. I think I'm going to call it 'Life Interrupted'."

"That's cool. Are you going to write about me and Sam?"

Before Claudie could answer, the front door opened and they could hear a miniature tornado scurrying down the hallway. Pooh shot into the kitchen and started doing figure eights around their feet. Sam was not far behind.

"Guess what we just learned to do at dog training school?" He dug a piece of kibble out of his pocket and held it over

Pooh's head. The dog reared up on his hind legs and pawed the air for the treat.

"I taught him to dance. Watch!" Sam walked around the room and Pooh followed without once setting his feet down on the floor. "And guess what? He's not a Pug—he's a Bug. The trainer said he was part French Bulldog and part Pug. I'm going to call him Pooh Bug."

"That's nice, Sam, now you and your bug go upstairs. I'm trying to bake a cake and I don't need you two underfoot."

No sooner were Sam and Pooh out of the way than the side door opened and Frank let himself in and went directly to the refrigerator for a beer.

"Maddie, what are you up to this fine day?"

"I'm making a cake, Uncle Frank. How are Gerlinda and the baby?"

"Gerlinda's mother is visiting. They're plotting ways to remodel Corrine's house. I'm superfluous to their plans. Good morning, Peter."

Peter came into the kitchen and poured a cup of coffee, noting one of his beers in Frank's hands. He glanced out the window and sure enough Frank had parked his car in the driveway, blocking his car in.

"Glad to hear that you're getting your vice-principal job back. Bet you're glad you won't have to dig idiots out of ditches next winter." Frank finished the beer and considered pulling another one out of the refrigerator but under Peter's watchful eyes he thought better of it.

"Thanks, Frank. I need you to move your car to the street. I need to get out."

"Sure. Claudie, I need that password."

Claudie gave him the password and he opened the door and left.

"Making a cake, Maddie?" Peter stood behind his daughter, reading the recipe she was working on.

"I'm going to try."

"I have some baking soda next door, Maddie. I'll give you some if you save me a piece of the cake."

"It'll probably be a disaster." Maddie made a glum face and her father gave her shoulder a reassuring squeeze before going outside.

"Well, success in cooking is a lot like life," Claudie said. "You have to go through a lot of failures before you get the hang of things. Trust me, this is one thing I know for sure."

Boy, did she know this. The last six months had been an amazing revelation to her. Life still had a host of surprises to throw at her and she was ready for them all. She couldn't wait.

The End

Acknowledgments

want to thank Ed Goldberg and Mary Rosenblum for all their encouragement on my writing. You made me feel I could honestly say 'writer' when someone asked me what I did. Still feels strange.

Thanks to everyone at Promontory Press for working so hard to bring this book to press. Special thanks to Ben Coles and Amy O'Hara for their support and gentle guidance.

About the Author

Jeanette Hubbard was born in Iowa and received her undergraduate degree in English at the University of Iowa, but has lived for so long in Oregon that she has certified web feet. For over twenty years she owned and ran a wholesale nursery west of Portland. She was relieved of that responsibility by the great recession. This gave her the gift of time she needed to pursue her dream of writing fiction. *Secrets, Lies and Champagne Highs* is her first published novel.

Her next book is a thriller with deliciously evil characters that sprang from a completely different area of her imagination. It will be published in the fall of 2015 under her pseudonym of J.R. Colbert.

www.jeanettehubbard.com